OH-SO-SENSIBLE
SECRETARY

OH-SO-SENSIBLE SECRETARY

BY

JESSICA HART

First published in Great Britain 2010
Large Print edition 2010
Harlequin Mills & Boon Limited,
Eton House, 18-24 Paradise Road,
Richmond, Surrey TW9 1SR

© Jessica Hart 2010

ISBN: 978 0 263 21226 6

Printed and bound in Great Britain
by CPI Antony Rowe, Chippenham, Wiltshire

For Nikki at 2DC,
with many thanks for all her work on the website

CHAPTER ONE

EVERYTHING was in place. A sleek computer sat on my desk, humming gently. A notebook and freshly sharpened pencil were squared up to one side of a high-tech phone, but otherwise the desk was empty, the way I like it. I can't bear clutter.

There was only one thing missing.

My new boss.

Phin Gibson was late, and I was cross. I can't bear unpunctuality either.

I had been there since eight-thirty. Wanting to make a good impression, I'd dressed carefully in my best grey checked suit, and my make-up was as subtle and professional as ever. Rattling over the keyboard, my nails had a perfect French manicure. I was only twenty-six, but anyone looking at me would know that I was the ultimate executive PA, cool, calm and capable.

I might have *looked* cool, but by half past ten

I certainly wasn't feeling it. I was irritated with Phin, and wishing I had bought myself a doughnut earlier.

Now, I know I don't look like the kind of girl with a doughnut fetish, but I can't get through the morning without a sugar fix. It's something to do with my metabolism (well, that's my story and I'm sticking to it), and if I don't have something sweet by eleven o'clock I get scratchy and irritable.

OK, even *more* irritable.

Chocolate or biscuits will do at a pinch, but doughnuts are my thing, and there's a coffee bar just round the corner from Gibson & Grieve's head office which sells the lightest, jammiest, sugariest ones I've ever tasted.

I'd fallen into the habit of buying one with a cappuccino on my way into work, and waiting for a quiet moment to get my blood sugar level up later in the morning, but today I'd decided not to. I wasn't sure what sort of boss Phin Gibson would prove to be, and I didn't want to be caught unawares with a sugar moustache or jammy fingers on our first day working together. This job was a big opportunity for me, and I wanted to impress him with my professionalism.

But how could I do that if he wasn't there?

Exasperated, I went back to my e-mail to Ellie, my friend in Customer and Marketing.

No problem, Ellie. To be honest, I was glad of something to do. There's a limit to what you can do as a PA without a boss—who STILL hasn't appeared, by the way. You'd think he could be bothered to turn up on time on his first day in a new job, but apparently not. Am already wishing I was back in the Chief Executive's office. I have a nasty feeling Phin and I aren't going to get on, and unless

——Original Message——
From: e.sanderson@gibsonandgrieve.co.uk
To: s.curtis@gibsonandgrieve.co.uk
Sent: Monday, January 18, 09:52
Subject: THANK YOU!

Summer, you are star! Thank you SO much for putting those figures together for me—and on a Friday afternoon, too! You saved my life (again!!!!!).

Any sign of Phin Gibson yet??? Can't

wait to hear if he's as gorgeous as he looks on telly!

Exx

'Well, well, well…Lex must know me better than I thought he did.'

The deep, amused voice broke across my exasperated typing and my head jerked up as I snatched my fingers back from the keyboard.

And there—at last!—was my new boss. Phinneas Gibson himself, lounging in the doorway and smiling the famously lop-sided smile that had millions of women, including my flatmate Anne, practically dribbling with lust.

I'd never dribbled myself. I'm not much of a dribbler at the best of times, and that oh-so-engaging smile smacked a little too much of I'm-incredibly-attractive-and-charming-and-don't-I-know-it for my taste.

My first reaction at the sight of Phin was one of surprise. No, thinking about it, surprise isn't quite the right word. I was *startled*.

I'd known what he looked like, of course. It would have been hard not to when Anne had insisted that I sit through endless repeats of *Into the Wild*. It's her flat, so she gets control of the remote.

If you're one of the two per cent of the population fortunate enough never to have seen it, Phin Gibson takes ill-assorted groups of people to the more inhospitable places on the planet, where they have to complete some sort of task in the most appalling conditions. On camera.

According to Anne, it makes for compulsive viewing, but personally I've never been able to see the point of making people uncomfortable just for sake of it. I mean, what's the point of hacking through a jungle when you can take a plane?

But don't get me started on reality TV. That's another thing I can't bear.

So I was braced against the extraordinary blue eyes, the shaggy dark blond hair and the smile, but I hadn't counted on how much bigger and more *immediate* Phin seemed in real life. Seeing him on the small screen gave no sense of the vivid impact of his presence.

I'm not sure I can explain it properly. You know that feeling when a gust of wind catches you unawares? When it swirls round you, sucking the air from your lungs and leaving you blinking and ruffled and invigorated? Well, that's what it felt like the first time I laid eyes on Phin Gibson.

There was a kind of lazy grace about him as he leant there, watching me with amusement. So it wasn't that he radiated energy. It was more that everything around him was energised by his presence. You could practically see the molecules buzzing in the air, and Phin himself seemed to be using up more than his fair share of oxygen in the room, which left me annoyingly short of breath.

Not that I was going to let Phin guess *that*.

'Good morning, Mr Gibson,' I said. Minimising the screen just in case, I took off the glasses I wear for working at the computer and offered a cool smile.

'Is it possible that *you're* my PA?' The blue eyes studied me with a mixture of surprise, amusement and appreciation as Phin levered himself away from the doorway and strolled into the room.

'I'm Summer Curtis, yes.'

A little miffed at his surprise, and ruffled by the amusement, I pushed back my chair so that

I could rise and offer my hand across the desk. *Some* of us were professional.

Phin's fingers closed around mine and he held onto my hand as he looked at me. 'Summer? No.'

'I'm afraid so,' I said a little tightly. I can't tell you how many times I've wished I was called something sensible, like Sue or Sarah, but never more than at that moment, with those blue eyes looking down into mine, filled with laughter.

I tried to withdraw my hand, but Phin was keeping a tight hold on it, and I was uncomfortably aware of the firm warmth of skin pressed against mine.

'You are *so* not a Summer,' he said. 'I've never met anyone with a more inappropriate name. Although I did know a girl called Chastity once, now I come to think of it,' he added. 'Look at you. Cool and crisp. Conker-brown hair. Eyes like woodsmoke. What were your parents thinking when they called you Summer instead of Autumn?'

'Not about how embarrassing it would be for me to go through life named after a season, anyway,' I said, managing to tug my hand free at last. I sat down again and rested it on the desk, where it throbbed disconcertingly.

'I must thank Lex,' said Phin. To add to my discomfort, he perched on my desk and turned sideways to look at me. 'He told me he'd appointed a PA for me, but I was expecting a dragon.'

'I can be a dragon if required,' I said, although right then I felt very undragon-like. I was suffocatingly aware of Phin on the other side of the desk. He wasn't anywhere near me, but his presence was still overwhelming. 'I'm fully qualified,' I added stiffly.

'I feel sure Lex wouldn't have appointed you if you weren't,' Phin said.

He had picked up my pencil and was twirling it absently between his fingers. It's the kind of fiddling that drives me mad, and I longed to snatch it from him, but I wasn't that much of a dragon.

'What's your brief?' he added, still twirling.

'Brief?'

The look he shot me was unexpectedly acute. 'Don't tell me Lex hasn't put you in here to keep an eye on me.'

I shifted uncomfortably.

'You're the most sensible person around here,' had been Lex Gibson's exact words when he offered me the job. 'I need someone competent to stop that idiot boy doing anything stupid. God knows what he'd get up to on his own!'

Not that I could tell Phin that. I admired Lex, but I wondered now if he was quite right. Phin didn't seem like an idiot to me, and he certainly wasn't a boy. He wasn't that much older than me—in his early thirties, perhaps—but he was clearly all man.

'Your brother thought it would be helpful for you to have an assistant who was familiar with the way the company operates,' I said carefully instead.

'In other words,' said Phin, interpreting this without difficulty, 'my brother thinks I'm a liability and wants you to keep me in order.'

I'd leapt at the chance of a promotion, even if it did mean working for Lex Gibson's feckless younger brother. Perhaps I should just explain, for those of you who have just jetted in from Mars—well, OK, from outside the UK—Gibson & Grieve is a long-established chain of department stores with a reputation for quality and style that others can only envy. The original, very exclusive store was in London, but now you'll find us in all the major British cities—setting a gold standard in retail, as Lex likes to say.

The Grieves died out long ago, but the Gibsons still have a controlling share, and Lex Gibson now runs the company with an iron hand. As far as I knew, Phin had never shown the slightest interest in Gibson & Grieve until now, but, as heir to a substantial part of it, he was automatically a member of the board. He was coming in right at the top, and that meant that his PA—me—would be working at the most senior level.

I gathered the idea was for Phin to spend a year as the public face of Gibson & Grieve, so even though the job wasn't permanent it would look very good on my CV. And the extra money wouldn't hurt, either. If I was ever going to be able to buy my own place I needed to save as much as I could, and this promotion would make quite a difference to my salary. I'm someone who likes to have a plan, and this job was a major step on my way. I might not be thrilled at the thought of working for Phin Gibson, but it wasn't an opportunity I was prepared to lose.

I couldn't dream about a future with Jonathan now, I remembered sadly, and that left buying my own flat the only plan I had. I mustn't jeopardise it by getting on the wrong side of Phin, no matter how irritatingly he fiddled.

'I'm your personal assistant,' I assured him. 'It's my job to support you. I'm here to do whatever you want.'

'Really?'

'Of course,' I began with dignity, then saw that his eyes were alight with laughter. To my chagrin, I felt a blush steal up my cheeks. It was just a pity my plan involved working with someone who was clearly incapable of taking anything seriously. 'Within reason, of course.'

'Oh, of *course*,' Phin agreed, eyes still dancing.

Then, much to my relief, he dropped the pencil and got up from the desk. 'Well, if we're going to be working together we'd better get to know each other properly, don't you think? Let's have some coffee.'

'Certainly.' Making coffee for my boss. That I could do. Pleased to be back in proper PA mode, I swung my chair round and got to my feet. 'I'll make some right away.'

'I don't want you to make it,' said Phin. 'I want to go out.'

'But you've just arrived,' I objected.

'I know, and I'm feeling claustrophobic already.' He looked around the office without enthusiasm. 'It's all so...sterile. Doesn't it make you want to shout obscenities and throw rubbish everywhere?'

I actually winced at the thought.

'No,' I said. Gibson & Grieve had always been noted for its style and up-market image. The offices were all beautifully designed and gleamed with the latest technology. I loved the fact that this one was light and spacious, and free as yet of any of the clutter that inevitably accumulated in a working office. 'I like everything neat and tidy,' I told Phin.

'You know, I should have been able to guess that,' he said in a dry voice, and I suddenly saw myself through his eyes: crisp and restrained in my grey suit, my hair fastened neatly back from my face. In comparison, he looked faintly unkempt, in jeans, a black T-shirt and a battered old leather jacket. He might look appropriate for a media meeting, but it was hardly appropriate for an executive director of a company like Gibson & Grieve, I thought disapprovingly.

Still, I had no doubt he was even less impressed by me. I would have bet on the fact that he thought me smart, but dull.

But then maybe all men thought that when they looked at me. Jonathan had, too, in the end.

I pushed the thought of Jonathan aside. 'We can go out if you'd rather,' I said. 'But don't you at least want to check your messages first?'

Phin's brows rose. 'I have messages?'

'Of course. You're a director and a board member,' I pointed out. 'We set up a new e-mail address for you last week, and you've been getting messages ever since. I'm able to filter them for you, and you have another address which only you will be able to access.'

'Great,' said Phin. 'Filtering sounds good to me. Is there anything important?'

'It's all important when you're a director.' I couldn't help the reproving note in my voice, but Phin only rolled his eyes.

'OK, is there anything *urgent*?'

I was forced to admit that there wasn't. 'Not really.'

'There you go,' he said cheerfully. 'I didn't think I'd need a PA, but Lex was right—as always. You've saved me wading through all those e-mails already. You deserve a coffee for that,' he told me, and held open the door for me. 'Come on, let's go.'

It was all going to be very different now, I thought, stifling a sigh as we headed down the corridor to the lift. I was used to working for Lex Gibson, who barely stopped working to sip the coffee Monique, his PA, took in to him.

Lex would never dream of going out for coffee, or bothering to get to know his secretaries, come to that. I was fairly sure he knew nothing about my private life. As far as Lex was concerned you were there to work, not to make friends, and I was perfectly happy with that. I didn't want to get all chummy with Phin, but for better or worse he was my boss now, so I could hardly refuse.

'Where's the best place for coffee round here?' Phin asked when we pushed through the revolving doors and out into the raw January morning. At least it wasn't raining for once, but I shivered in my suit, wishing I'd bothered to throw on my coat after all.

'Otto's is very good,' I said, hugging my arms together. 'It's just round the corner.'

'Better and better,' said Phin. 'Lead the way.' He glanced down at me, shivering as we waited to cross the road. 'You look cold. Would you like to borrow my jacket?'

The thought of his jacket, warm from his body, slung intimately around my shoulders, was strangely disturbing—quite apart from the fact that it would look very odd with my suit. 'I'm fine, thank you,' I said, clenching my teeth to stop them chattering.

'Let's step on it, then,' he said briskly. 'It's freezing.'

The warmth and the mouth-watering smell of freshly baked pastries enveloped us as we pushed through the door into Otto's. Inside it was dark and narrow, with four old-fashioned booths on one side and some stools at a bar in the window.

The coffee and sandwiches were so good that first thing in the morning and at lunchtime there was always a long queue out of the door, but it was relatively quiet now. We lined up behind three executives exuding testosterone as they compared bonuses, a German tourist, and a pair of middle-aged women carrying on a conversation that veered bizarrely between some terrible crisis that a mutual friend was enduring and whether a Danish pastry was more or less fattening than a blueberry muffin.

Phin picked up a tray and hustled me along behind them. 'What about something to eat?' he said. 'I'm going to have something. I'm starving.'

I eyed the doughnuts longingly, but there was no way I was going to eat one in front of him. 'Just coffee, please.'

'Sure?' I could almost believe he had seen the yearning in my eyes, because he leant suggestively towards me. 'You don't want a piece of that chocolate cake?' he said, rolling the words around his mouth suggestively. 'A scone with cream? One of those pastries? Go on—you know you want to!'

I gritted my teeth. 'No, thank you.'

'Well, you're a cheap date,' he said. 'I'm going to have one of those doughnuts.'

I had to press my lips firmly together to stop myself whimpering.

Ahead, Otto's ferocious wife, Lucia, was making coffee, shouting orders back to Otto, and working the till with her customary disregard for the service ethic. Lucia was famous for her rudeness and the customers were all terrified of her. I've seen senior executives reduced to grovelling if they didn't have the correct change. If the coffee and the cakes hadn't been so good, or if Lucia hadn't been so efficient, Otto's would have closed long ago. As it was, she and the café had become something of a local institution.

'Next!' she snarled as we made it to the top of the queue, and then she caught sight of me and smiled—a sight so rare that the executives now helping themselves to sugar stared in disbelief.

'Back again, *cara*?' she called, banging out old coffee grounds from the espresso machine. 'Your usual?'

'Yes, thanks, Lucia.' I smiled back at her, and then glanced at Phin, who was watching me with an oddly arrested expression. 'And…?' I prompted him.

'Americano for me,' he supplied quickly, before Lucia got impatient with him. 'No milk.'

'Why are you looking at me like that?' I asked Phin as I slid onto a shiny plastic banquette. Otto's wasn't big on style.

'I'm curious,' he said, transferring the cups to the table and pushing the tray aside.

'Curious?'

'Perhaps intrigued is a better word,' said Phin. 'You know, I've dodged guerrillas in South America, I've been charged at by a rhino and dangled by a rope over a thousand-foot crevasse, but I found Lucia pretty scary. She had every single person in that queue intimidated, but you she calls *cara*. What's that about?'

'Oh, nothing,' I said, making patterns in the cappuccino froth with my teaspoon. 'I wrote her a note once, that was all.'

'What sort of note?'

'I noticed that she wasn't here one day, mainly because the queue doesn't move nearly as fast when she's not around. I asked why not, and she told me she'd had to go back to Italy because her father had died. I wrote her a short note, just to say that I was sorry. It wasn't a big deal,' I muttered. I was rather embarrassed by the way Lucia had never forgotten it.

Phin looked at me thoughtfully. 'That was a kind thing to do.'

Feeling awkward, I sipped at my coffee. 'I

didn't do much,' I said. 'Anyone can write a note.'

'But only you did.'

He picked up his doughnut and took a big bite while I watched enviously. My mouth was watering, and I was feeling quite light-headed with the lack of sugar.

'Want a bit?' he asked, offering the plate.

I flushed at the thought that he had noticed me staring. 'No...thank you,' I said primly.

'Sure? It's very good.'

I *knew* it was good. That was the trouble. 'I'm sure.'

'Suit yourself.' Phin shrugged, and finished the doughnut with unnecessary relish.

The more he enjoyed it, the crosser I got. What sort of boss was this, who dragged you out to coffee, tried to force-feed you doughnuts and then tortured you by eating them in front of you?

Scowling, I buried my face in my cappuccino.

'So, Summer Curtis,' he said, brushing sugar from his fingers at last. 'Tell me about yourself.'

It sounded like an interview question, so I sat up straighter and composed myself. 'Well, I've been working for Gibson & Grieve for five years now, the last three as assistant to the Chief Executive's PA—' I began, but Phin held up both hands.

'I don't need to know how many A levels you've got or where you've worked,' he said. 'I'm sure Lex wouldn't have appointed you if he didn't trust you absolutely. I'm more interested in finding out what makes you tick. If you're going to be my personal assistant I think we should get to know each other personally, and your work experience won't tell me anything I really need to know.'

'Like what?' I asked, disconcerted.

Phin sat back against the banquette and eyed me thoughtfully. 'Like your pet peeves, for instance. What really irritates you?'

'How long have you got?' I asked. 'Sniffing. Jiggling. Mess. Smiley faces made out of punctuation marks. Phrases like "Ah…bless…" or "I love her to bits, but…" Men who sit on the tube with their legs wide apart. Unpunctuality. Sloppy spelling and misuse of the apostrophe—that's a big one for me.' I paused, aware that I might have been getting a bit carried away. 'Do you want me to go on?'

'I think I might be getting the picture,' he said, his mouth twitching.

'I'm a bit of a perfectionist.'

'So I gathered.' I could tell he was trying not to laugh, and I was beginning to regret being so honest.

'You did ask,' I pointed out defensively.

'I did. Maybe I should have asked you what you *do* like.'

'I like my job.'

'Being a secretary?'

I nodded. 'Organisations like Gibson & Grieve don't work unless executives have proper administrative back-up. I like organising things, checking details, pulling everything together. I like making sure everything is in its right place. That's why I like filing. I find it satisfying.'

Phin didn't say anything. He just looked at me across the table.

'I'm sorry,' I said, putting up my chin. 'I do. Shoot me.'

He grinned at that. 'So…an unexpectedly kind, nitpicking perfectionist with an irrational prejudice against poor punctuation and a bizarre attachment to filing. I think we're getting somewhere. What else do I need to know about you?'

'Nothing.'

'Nothing? There must be more than that.'

I drank my coffee, unaccountably flustered. I was more thrown than I wanted to admit by the blueness of his eyes, by that lazy smile and the sheer vitality of his presence. There was a whole table between us, but I was finding it hard to breathe.

'I really don't know what you want me to tell you,' I said. 'I'm twenty-six, I share a flat in south London with a friend, and my life is the exact opposite of yours.'

His eyes gleamed at that, and he leant forward. 'What do you mean?'

'Well, you come from a wealthy family whose stores are a household name,' I pointed out. 'You make television programmes doing the kind of things the rest of us would never dare to do, and when you're not skiing down a glacier or hacking through a jungle you're at all the A-list parties—usually with a beautiful girl on your arm. The closest *I* get to an A-list party is reading about one in *Glitz*, and I'd rather stick pins in my eyes than set foot in a rainforest. We don't have a single thing in common.'

'You can't say that,' Phin objected. 'You don't really know anything about me.'

'I feel as if I do,' I told him. 'My flatmate, Anne, is your biggest fan, and after listening to her talk about you for the past two years I could take a quiz on you myself.' I pushed my empty cup aside. 'Go on—ask me. Anything,' I offered largely, and even gave him an example. 'What's your latest girlfriend called?'

A smile was tugging at the corner of Phin's mouth. 'You tell me,' he said.

'Jewel,' I said triumphantly. 'Jewel Stevens. She's an actress, and when you went to some awards ceremony last week she wore a red dress that had Anne weeping with envy.'

'But not you?'

'I think it would have looked classier in black,' I said, and Phin laughed.

'I'm impressed. Clearly I don't need to tell you anything about myself, as you know it all already. Although I think I should point out that Jewel *isn't*, in fact, my girlfriend. We've been out a couple of times, but that's all. There's no question of a real relationship, whatever the papers say.'

'I'll tell Anne. She'll be delighted,' I said. 'She's got a very active fantasy life in which you figure largely, in spite of the fact that she's very happy with her fiancé, Mark.'

'And what do you fantasise about, Summer?' asked Phin, his eyes on my face.

Ah, my fantasies. They were always the same. Jonathan realising that he had made a terrible mistake. Jonathan telling me he loved me. Jonathan asking me to marry him. We'd buy a house together. London prices being what they were, we might have to go out to the suburbs, and even pooling our resources we'd be lucky to get a semi-detached house, but that would be fine by me. I didn't need anywhere grand. I just wanted Jonathan, and somewhere I could stay.

I realise a suburban semi-detached isn't the stuff of most wild fantasies, but it was a dream that had kept me going ever since Jonathan had told me before Christmas that he 'needed some space'. He thought it was better that we didn't see each other outside the office any more. He knew how sensible I was, and was sure I would understand.

I sighed. What could I do but agree that, yes,

I understood? But I lived for the brief glimpses I had of him now, and the hope that he might change his mind.

Phin was watching me expectantly, his brows raised, and I had an uneasy sense that those blue eyes could see a lot more than they ought to be able to. He was still waiting for me to answer his question.

Jonathan had been insistent that we keep our relationship a secret at the office, so I hadn't told anyone. I certainly wasn't going to start with Phin Gibson.

'I want a place of my own,' I said. 'It doesn't have to be very big—in fact I'll be lucky if I can afford a studio—but it has to be mine. It has to be somewhere I could live for ever.' I glanced at him. 'I suppose you think that's very boring?'

'It's not what I was expecting, and it's not a fantasy I understand, but it's not *boring*,' said Phin. 'I don't find much boring, to tell you the truth. People are endlessly interesting, don't you think? Obviously not!' he went straight on, seeing my sceptical expression. 'Well, *I* find them interesting. Why is it so important for you to have a home of your own?'

'Oh...I moved around a lot as a child. My mother has always been heavily into alternative lifestyles, and she's prone to sudden intense enthusiasms. One year we'd be in a commune, the next we were living on a houseboat. When my father was alive we had a couple of freezing years in a tumbledown smallholding in Wales.'

It was odd to find myself telling Phin Gibson, of all people, about my childhood. I didn't normally talk about it much—not that it had been particularly traumatic, but it was hard for most people I knew to understand what it was like growing up with a mother who was as charming and lovely and flaky as they come—and there was something about the way he was listening, his expression intent and his attention absolutely focused on me, that unlocked my usual reserve.

'Wales was the closest we ever got to settling down,' I told him. 'The rest of the time we kept moving. Not because we had to, but because my mother was always looking for something more.

'Basically,' I said, 'she's got the attention span of a gnat. I lost count of the schools I attended, of the weird and wonderful places we lived for a few months before moving on.'

I turned the cup and saucer between my fingers. 'I suppose it's inevitable I grew up craving security the way others crave excitement. My mother can't understand it, though. She's living in a tepee in Somerset at the moment, and for her the thought of buying a flat and settling down is incomprehensible. I'm a big disappointment to her,' I finished wryly.

'There you are—we've something in common after all,' said Phin, sitting back with a smile and stretching his long legs out under the table. 'I'm a big disappointment to my parents, too.'

CHAPTER TWO

I LOOKED at him in surprise. 'But you're famous,' I said. I'd known Lex wasn't impressed by his younger brother, but had assumed that his parents at least would be pleased by his success. 'You've had a successful television career.'

'My parents aren't impressed by television.' Phin smiled wryly. 'They think the media generally is shallow and frivolous—certainly compared to the serious business of running Gibson & Grieve. Lex and I were brought up to believe that the company was all that mattered, and that it was the only future we could ever have or ever want.'

'When did you change your mind?'

'When I realised that there wasn't really a place for me here. Lex is older than me, and anyway he had Chief Executive written all over him even as a toddler. Gibson & Grieve was all he ever cared about.'

It was my turn to study Phin. He was looking quite relaxed, leaning back against the banquette, but I sensed that this wasn't an easy topic of conversation for him.

'Didn't you ever want to be part of it, too?'

'As a very small boy I used to love going into the office,' he admitted. 'But as I got bigger I didn't fit. I was always being told to be quiet or sit still, and I didn't like doing either of those things. I wanted to skid over the shiny floors, or play football, or fiddle with the new computers. After a while I stopped going.'

Phin's smile was a little crooked. 'Of course it's easy now to see that I was just a spoilt brat looking for attention, but at the time it felt as if I were reacting against all their expectations. Lex was always there, doing what he should, and there never seemed any point in me doing the same. I got into as much trouble as I could instead,' he said. 'My parents were beside themselves. They didn't know what to do with me, and I didn't know what to do with myself. I don't think they ever thought I would get a degree, and I took off as soon as I'd graduated. I suspect that they were glad to be rid of me! I mean, what would they have done with me at Gibson & Grieve? I didn't fit with the image at all!'

No, he wouldn't have done, I thought. In spite of its commitment to style, Gibson & Grieve was at heart a very solid, traditional company— it was one of the reasons I liked it—and Phin would have been too chaotic, too vibrant, too energetic to ever properly fit in.

'So what did you do?' I asked, wondering how he was going to fit in now that he was back.

'I messed around for a few years,' he said. 'I worked my way around the world. I didn't care what I did as long as I was somewhere I could keep my adrenalin pumping—skiing, sailing, white-water rafting, climbing, sky-diving…I tried them all. I spent some time in the Amazon and learnt jungle survival skills, and then I got a job leading a charity expedition, and that led onto behind the scenes advice on a reality TV programme.'

He shrugged. 'It seems I came across well on camera, and the next thing I knew they'd offered me my own programme, taking ill-assorted groups into challenging situations.'

And I knew what had happened after that. It had taken no time at all for Phin Gibson to become a celebrity, almost as famous as Gibson & Grieve itself.

'And now you've joined the company,' I said.

'I have.' Phin was silent for a moment, looking down at his hands, which lay lightly clasped on the table, and then he looked up at me and the blueness of his eyes was so intense that I actually drew a sharp breath.

'Last year I took a group of young offenders on a gruelling trek through Peru,' he said.

I remembered the programme. I had watched it with Anne, and even I had had to admit that the change in those boys by the end of the trek was extraordinary.

'I recognised myself in them,' Phin said. 'It made me think about how difficult it must have been for my parents. I guess I'd grown up in spite of myself.'

His mouth quirked in a self-deprecating grin, then he sobered. 'My father had a stroke last year as well. That put a new perspective on everything. It seemed to me that it was time to try and make some amends. My mother has got it into her mind that all Dad wants is for me to settle down and take up my inheritance at Gibson & Grieve.'

He sighed a little. 'To be honest, it's a little hard to know exactly what Dad wants now, but he did manage to squeeze my hand when my mother told him what she had in mind. Basically, a certain amount of emotional blackmail is being applied! In lots of ways it's worse for Lex,' Phin went on thoughtfully. 'He stepped into my father's shoes as Chief Executive, and he's been doing a good job. Profits are up. Everyone's happy. The last thing he wants is me muddying the waters. In the end he suggested that we capitalise on my "celebrity", for want of better word, and make me the new face of Gibson & Grieve. You know we've just acquired Gregson's?'

He cocked an eyebrow at me and I nodded. The acquisition had made the headlines a few months ago when it happened.

'Supermarkets are a change of direction for us,' Phin went on. 'Our brand has always been up-market, even exclusive, and we need more of a popular, family-friendly image now. Lex seems to think I can help with that, and I agreed to see how it went for a year initially, on condition that I could finish a couple of filming commitments.'

I smoothed my skirt over my knees. I was feeling a bit bad, if you want the truth. I'd dismissed Phin as a spoilt celebrity and assumed that he was choosing to dabble in the family business for a while. I hadn't realised that he was under some pressure.

'It makes sense for you to be Director of Media Relations,' I offered.

'I think we all know how little that means,' said Phin, leaning across the table, and I found myself leaning back as if pushed there by the sheer force of his personality. 'Lex's idea is to shunt me off and just wheel me out to be photographed every now and then. As far as he's concerned all the media relations will be done by his PR guy…what's his name? John?'

'Jonathan Pugh.'

Just saying his name was enough to bump my heart into my throat, and my tongue felt thick and unwieldy in my mouth. I wondered if Phin would notice how husky I sounded, but he didn't seem to.

'Yep, that's him,' was all he said, sitting back again. 'A born suit.'

I bridled at the dismissive note in his voice. I'd been quite liking Phin until then, but I was very sensitive to any criticism of Jonathan. At least Jonathan dressed professionally, unlike *some* people I could mention, I thought, eyeing Phin's T-shirt disapprovingly.

'Jonathan's very good at his job,' I said stiffly.

'Lex wouldn't employ him unless he was,' said Phin. 'But if he's that good there won't be much left for me to do, will there? I'm not going to spend a year opening stores and saving Lex the trouble of turning up at charity bashes.'

'Then why come back if you're not going to do anything?' I asked, still ruffled by his dismissal of Jonathan.

'But I am going to do something,' he said. 'Lex just doesn't know it yet. If I'm going to be part of Gibson & Grieve, I'm going to make a difference.'

Oh, dear. I had a nasty feeling this was the kind of thing Lex had meant when he had told me to stop Phin doing anything stupid.

'How?' I asked warily.

'By increasing our range of fair trade products. Promoting links with communities here and overseas. Being more aware of environmental issues. Developing our staff and providing more training. Making *connections*,' said Phin. 'We're all part of chain. It doesn't matter if we're picking tea in Sri Lanka, stacking it on the shelves in Sheffield or buying it in Swindon. We should be celebrating the connections between people, not pretending that the only thing that matters is underlying operating profit or consensus forecasts.'

I was secretly impressed that Phin even knew about consensus forecasts, but I couldn't see any of this going down well with Lex.

I nibbled my thumb. It's a bad habit of mine when I'm unsure. 'And you haven't discussed any of this with your brother yet?'

'Not yet, no,' he said. 'I wanted to get to know you first.'

'Me?' I was taken aback. 'Why?'

'Because if I'm going to get anything done I need a team. I need to be sure that we can work together, and that we share the same goals.'

The blue, blue eyes fixed on me with that same unnerving intensity. 'You've been working for Lex, and I know his staff are all very loyal to him. I'm not trying to take over, but there's no use pretending he's going to share my ideas, and I don't want to put you in a difficult position. If you'd rather not work with me to change things, this is the time to say, Summer. I'm sure Lex would give you your old job back if you wanted it, and there'd be no hard feelings.'

I'll admit it. I hesitated. There was part of me that longed to go back to the Chief Executive's office—which buzzed with drive, where everyone was cool and efficient, and where there was no Phin Gibson with his unsettling presence and alarming ideas about change. I didn't like change. I'd had enough of change as a child. I wanted everything to stay the same.

But this was my big chance. When Anne got married I was going to have to move out of the flat. With my new salary I might be able to save enough to put down a deposit on a place of my own by then. It was only for a year, too, I reminded myself. When it was up, I'd be in a good position to get another job at the same level in spite of my age. It would be worth putting up with Phin until then.

So I met the blue eyes squarely. 'I don't want my old job back,' I said. 'I want to be part of your team.'

I was sorting through the post the next morning when Phin appeared. Late again. Hadn't he ever heard of a nine-to-five day at work?

He had spent no more than a couple of hours in the office after we had got back from Otto's, before disappearing to a meeting with his producer.

'But I've read all my e-mails, you'll be glad to hear,' he said as he left. 'I take back everything I said about never being bored. All that corporate jargon puts me to sleep faster than a cup of cocoa. I'm never going to make it through a meeting if these guys actually talk like that.'

It would be nice to think he would ever be there to *go* to a meeting, I thought crossly.

It was after ten, and I had been in a dilemma about when to have the doughnut I'd bought earlier at Otto's. Having forgone my treat the day before, I was determined not to miss out again, but I wanted a few minutes to myself, so that I could enjoy it properly. I needed Phin to be in his office, so that I knew where he was.

Not knowing when he might appear had been making me twitchy, so when Phin strolled in and wished me a cheerful good morning I glared at him over the top of my glasses.

'Where have you been?' I demanded.

'You know,' Phin confided, 'that librarian thing you've got going really works for me.'

'What librarian thing?' I asked, thrown.

'The fierce glasses on the chain, the scraped back hair, the neat suit…' He grinned at my expression, which must have been dumbfounded. That's certainly how I felt. 'Please say you're about to shake out your hair and tell me you're going to have to be very strict with me for being late!'

I'd never met anyone like Phin before, and I was completely flummoxed. 'What on earth are you talking about?'

'Never mind,' he said. 'I was just getting a bit carried away there. What was it you wanted to know again?'

'I was wondering where you'd been,' I said tightly. 'It's after ten. I was expecting you here an hour ago at least.'

'I went into the Oxford Street store to see how

things are going,' said Phin casually, picking up the post from my desk and leafing idly through it. 'I thought it would be an idea to meet the staff and hear what they think, and it was very useful.' He looked up at me, his eyes disconcertingly blue and amused. 'Why? Should I have asked permission?'

I pressed my lips together. 'It's not a question of permission,' I said. 'But there's no point in having a PA unless you let me know where you are. I need to be able to make appointments for you, and I can't do that if I've no idea when you're going to turn up.'

'Who wants an appointment?'

'Well, no one, as it happens,' I was forced to admit. 'But they might have done. It's a matter of principle.'

'Principle? That sounds serious.' Phin dropped the post back onto the desk and without thinking I squared up the pile, looking up when he sucked in his breath alarmingly.

'What's the matter?' I asked, startled.

'I don't know…' He was squinting at the pile I'd tidied. 'I think those papers at the bottom might be half a millimetre out of alignment.'

'Sarcasm—excellent,' I said. Sarcastically. That was all I needed. 'Thank you so much.'

He held up his hands. 'It's nothing, honestly. Just one more service we offer.'

My lips tightened. I tried to pick up the conversation. 'Perhaps we should agree a system.'

'A system,' said Phin, testing the word as if he'd never heard it before. 'Fine. What sort of system?'

'If you let me have your mobile number, so that I can get hold of you if I need to, that would be a start. And then perhaps we could sit down and go through your diary.'

'Absolutely. Let's do it.' He clenched his fist and punched it in the air, to demonstrate an enthusiasm I was perfectly aware he didn't feel. 'Let's do it now, in fact.'

'Fine.'

We exchanged mobile numbers, and then I carried the diary into his office. I would put all the details on the computer later, but it was easier at this stage to use an old-fashioned hard copy.

I sat down with the diary on my knee, while Phin fished out a personal organiser and leaned back in his chair so that he could prop his feet on the desk.

'What do you want to know?'

'I'd better have everything.' I smoothed the page open, admiring in passing how nice my hands looked. I take care of my nails, and today they were painted a lovely pale pink called Dew at Dawn. 'If you're the face of Gibson & Grieve, you'll be expected to appear at various functions and I'll need to know when you're available.'

'Fair enough.'

He had an extraordinarily complicated social life, with two or three events an evening as far as I could make out. I couldn't help comparing it with my own , which largely consisted of painting my nails in front of the television, watching Anne getting ready to go out with Mark and feeling miserable about Jonathan.

'This is great,' said Phin when we'd finished. 'I never need to remember anything by myself ever again. Maybe I won't mind being an executive after all. What else is there to do?'

'There's a meeting to discuss the new media strategy at half past ten,' I said, handing him a folder. 'Your brother suggested you went along if you were here on time. I've noted all the salient points, and included copies of recent minutes so you know the background.'

'Salient points?' he echoed, amazed. 'I didn't realise people still said things like that any more!'

I chose to ignore that, and looked pointedly at my watch instead. 'You should get going. You've only got a couple of minutes and you don't want to be late.'

'You mean *you* don't want me to be late,' said Phin, but he swung his legs down from the desk.

I could hardly wait for him to go. I practically shoved him out of the door towards the lifts. Lex's office was on the floor above, and as soon as I saw him step into the lift I scurried down the corridor to the kitchen to make myself some coffee.

My office, and Phin's of course, was in a prime location on the corner of the building, with fabulous views of Trafalgar Square, but more importantly we were at the end of the corridor, which meant that nobody dropped in just because they were passing.

Even so, I closed the door as a precaution and prepared to enjoy my doughnut in private. I settled happily behind my desk with my coffee and cleared a space. Eating a doughnut could be a messy business. Perhaps that was why it always felt faintly naughty to me.

At last. I pulled out the doughnut and took a bite, mumbling with pleasure as my teeth sank into the sugary dough.

And then froze as the door opened and Phin came in. 'I forgot that file—' he began, and then it was his turn to stop as he took in the sight of me, sitting guiltily behind my desk, doughnut in hand and mouth full.

His eyes lit with amusement. 'Aha! Caught red-handed, I see.'

Blushing furiously, I dropped the doughnut and brushed at the sugar moustache I could feel on my top lip. 'I thought you'd gone,' I blustered, mortified at having been caught in such an un-professional pose.

'Now I know why you were so keen to get rid of me,' said Phin. 'This is a new side to you. How very, very unlikely. Who would have thought that sensible Summer Curtis would have a doughnut addiction!' He leant conspiratorially towards me. 'Does anyone else know?'

'It's not an *addiction*,' I said, trying for some

dignity. 'I just work better if I've had some sugar in the morning.'

'Well, I'm delighted to find that you've got a weakness. I was finding all that perfection just a little intimidating.' He grinned. 'It's good to know that when it comes down to it you can't resist temptation either.'

Of course, then I had to prove him wrong.

The next day, when I called in to buy my usual cappuccino on my way into work, I refused the doughnut Lucia offered and felt virtuous. This would be the start of a new regime, I vowed. I didn't need a sugar fix, anyway. That was just silly. I would stick to coffee—a much less embarrassing habit and one that was less likely to lead to humiliation.

And I made it all the way to the lifts before I started to regret my resolution. Why shouldn't I have a mid-morning snack? It wasn't as if eating a doughnut was immoral or illegal. I blamed Phin for making me feel guilty about it. It was more satisfying than blaming myself.

Already I could already feel the craving twitching away in the pit of my stomach, making me tense. It didn't bode well for the rest of the day, and I hoped everyone would give me a wide berth. I wasn't known for my easygoing attitude on the best of days, and I had a feeling this most definitely wasn't going to be a good one.

At least Phin managed to turn up before ten o'clock, looking distinctly the worse for wear.

'I hope I get a gold star for turning up early,' he said.

I thinned my lips, still illogically determined to blame him for my doughnut-less day. 'I'd hardly call ten *early*,' I said repressively.

'It is for me.' Phin yawned. 'I had a very late night.'

I wondered how much his lack of sleep was due to the beautiful Jewel Stevens. According to last night's *Metro*, the two of them were 'inseparable'. Not that I was scouring gossip columns for news of my new boss, you understand. In spite of taking a book to read on the tube every day, I somehow always ended up devouring the free paper on the way home. When it's pressed into your hand, it seems rude not to.

Phin's name just happened to catch my eye— honest. There had even been a picture of him at some party, with Jewel entwined around his arm. I know I'm in no position to talk about stupid names, but really…Jewel? I'd put money on the fact that she was christened Julie. In the picture Phin had a faintly wary look, but that might have been the flash. He certainly didn't look as if he were pushing her away.

Why would he? She was dark and sultry, with legs up to her armpits, a beestung mouth and masses of rippling black hair. Every man's fantasy, in fact.

I felt vaguely depressed at the thought, and then worried by the fact that I was depressed— until I realised it must just be the lack of sugar getting to me.

'No, really, though. I'll be fine,' said Phin, when I failed to offer the expected sympathy. 'There's no need to make a fuss.'

I sighed and narrowed my eyes at him.

'I can tell that deep down you're really worried,' he said, and when I just looked back at him without expression he wisely took himself off into his office.

'I'll survive,' he promised, just before he shut the door. 'But if I don't, you're not to feel bad, OK?'

All was quiet for nearly an hour. I was betting that he had gone to catch up on his sleep on one of those sofas, but frankly I was glad to get rid of him for a while. I tried to soothe myself with a little filing, but a few days wasn't long enough to generate much of a backlog, and I couldn't stop thinking about how good a doughnut would taste with a cup of coffee.

Perhaps Phin was right. Perhaps I really was addicted, I fretted. I even considered sneaking out to Otto's, but couldn't take the chance of Phin waking up and finding me gone. I'd never hear the end of it.

The more I tried not to think about doughnuts, the more I wanted one, and it was almost a relief when Phin buzzed me. Yes, buzzed me—like a real executive! Maybe he would get the hang of corporate life after all.

'It's almost eleven,' came his voice through the intercom. 'Am I allowed to have coffee yet?'

'Of course,' I said, glad of the distraction from my doughnut craving, and relieved to be able to act as a normal PA for a change. 'I'll bring you some in.'

'Bring yourself some, too. We need to do some planning. You'll like that.'

Planning. That sounded more like it. I switched my phone through, wedged my notebook under my arm, and took in a pot of coffee and two cups on a tray.

I half expected to find Phin lying on one of the sofas, but he was sitting behind his desk, apparently immersed in something he was reading on the computer screen. He looked up when I pushed open the door with my elbow, though, and got to his feet.

'Let's make ourselves comfortable,' he said, guiding me over to the sofas and producing a familiar-looking paper bag from a drawer. 'I thought we'd have a little something with our coffee,' he said, waving it under my nose.

He'd brought two doughnuts.

It was all I could do not to drool. I've no idea what my expression was like, but judging by the laughter in the blue eyes it was a suitable picture.

'*Now* aren't you sorry you weren't more sympathetic?' he asked as he set the doughnuts out on a paper napkin each.

I eyed them longingly. 'I've just decided to give them up,' I said, but Phin only clicked his tongue.

'You can't do that just when I've found a weakness I can ruthlessly exploit,' he said. 'Besides, you told me yourself you needed a sugar fix in order to concentrate. You'll just get grumpy otherwise.'

Unfortunately that was all too true.

'Take it as an order, if that helps,' he said as I hesitated. 'Keeping me company on the doughnut front is compulsory. If I'd been able to appoint my own PA I'd have put it in the job description.'

What could I do? 'Well, if you insist…' I said, giving in.

I sat on one sofa, Phin sat on the other, and we bit into our doughnuts at the same time.

I can't tell you how good mine tasted. I laughed as I licked sugar from my fingers. 'Mmm…yum-yum,' I said, and then stopped as I saw Phin's arrested expression. 'What?'

'Nothing. I was just realising I hadn't heard you laugh yet,' he said. 'You should do it more often.

My eyes slid away from his. 'It's easy to laugh when you're being force-fed doughnuts,' I said after a tiny pause. I was very aware of him watching me, and I licked sugar from my lips with the tip of my tongue, suddenly uncomfortable as the silence stretched.

I cleared my throat. 'What exactly did you want to plan?' I said.

'Plan?' echoed Phin, sounding oddly distracted.

'You said we needed to do some planning,' I reminded him.

'Oh, yes…' He seemed to recover himself. 'Well, I had a chat about my role here with Lex last night, and we discussed things in a civilised manner.'

'Really?'

'No, not really. We had a knock-down-drag-out fight, and shouted at each other for a good hour. It didn't quite come to fisticuffs, but it was touch and go at one point. Just like being boys again,' he said reflectively.

I couldn't imagine anyone daring to shout at Lex, but then Phin was a self-confessed adrenalin junkie and obviously thrived on danger.

'What happened?' I asked a little nervously. I hoped Phin hadn't enraged his brother so much that we would be both be out of a job.

'I'd like to claim utter victory, but I'd be lying,' Phin admitted. 'Lex wasn't budging when it came to renegotiating our suppliers, but he did agree eventually that I could start to build up links with communities overseas. In return I had to promise to co-operate fully on the PR front. Apparently he's lined up a feature in *Glitz* already.'

Phin shrugged as he finished his doughnut and brushed the sugar from his hands. 'So, not everything I wanted, I'll admit, but it's a start.'

'Well…good,' I said, feeling a little uncertain. 'What happens next?'

'We'd better keep Lex quiet about the PR,' he decided. 'Make arrangements for that interview, and talk to Jonathan Pugh about what they want.'

Talk to Jonathan! *Talk to Jonathan.* My stomach clenched with excitement. I had a reason to go and talk to Jonathan! My handwriting was ridiculously shaky as I made a note, although there was no chance of me forgetting that particular task.

Phin was talking about a trip to Cameroon he was planning but I hardly listened. I was too busy imagining my meeting with Jonathan.

This would be my first chance to talk to him

properly since that awful evening when he had told me it 'wasn't working' for him. I had seen him around the office, of course, but never alone, and I was sure that he was avoiding me. I'd been holding onto the hope that if we could just spend some time together again he would change his mind.

I would play it cool, of course, I decided. Surely he knew that I was the last person to make a fuss? I would be calm and reasonable and undemanding. What more could he want? *I've missed you, Summer,* I imagined him saying as the scales dropped from his eyes and he realised that I was just what he needed after all. *You've no idea how much.*

But if he had missed me, why hadn't he told me? I puzzled over that one. OK, maybe he had just been waiting for the right moment. Or he'd thought I was busy.

It even sounded lame in my fantasy, which wasn't a good sign.

I suddenly realised that Phin had stopped talking and was looking at me enquiringly. 'So what do you think?' he asked.

'Um…sounds good to me,' I said hastily,

without a clue as to what he'd been talking about. 'Great idea.'

His brows lifted in surprise. 'Well, that's good. To be honest, I didn't think you'd go for it.'

'Oh?' I regarded him warily. That sounded ominous. 'Er…what exactly didn't you think I'd like?'

'Staff development in Cameroon,' he prompted, but his eyes had started to dance.

'What?'

Phin tried to look severe, but a smile tugged at the corner of his mouth. 'Summer, is it possible you weren't listening to a word I was saying?'

I squirmed. 'I may have got distracted there for a moment or two,' I admitted feebly.

He tutted. 'That's not like you, Summer. After I gave you sugar, too! I've just explained about my plan to take a group from Head Office to Cameroon for a couple of weeks, to help build a medical centre in one of the villages I know there. It's a great way to start forging links between the company and a community, and everyone who goes will get so much out of it. But you don't need to worry about it yet. You'll have plenty of time to prepare.'

'Hold on,' I said, alarmed by the way this was going. 'Me? Prepare for what?'

'Of course you'll be coming, too,' said Phin, with what I was sure was malicious pleasure in my consternation. 'We're a team, remember? This is our scheme. It's important that you're really part of it. What better way than to go as part of the first group, to find out what it's like out there?'

CHAPTER THREE

'YOU'RE not serious?'

'I'm always serious, Summer,' said Phin. His face was perfectly straight, but I've never seen anything less serious than the expression in the blue eyes right then.

I stared at him, aghast. 'No way am I going to Africa!'

'Why on earth not?'

'I don't like bugs.'

'There's more to the rainforest than bugs, Summer.'

'The rainforest?' My eyes started from my head. How much had I missed here? 'Oh, no. No, no, no. The jungle? No way. Absolutely not.'

'You'd like it.'

'I wouldn't,' I said, still shaking my head firmly from side to side. I'd seen him leading those poor people through enough rainforests on *Into the Wild* to know just what it would be like. They spent their whole time struggling through rampant vegetation, or slithering down muddy slopes in stifling humidity, so that their hair was plastered to their heads and their shirts wringing with sweat.

There was almost always a shot of Phin taking off his shirt and rinsing it in the water. Anne's favourite bit, in fact. Whenever they reached a river she'd sit up straighter and call out, 'Shirt alert!' and sigh gustily at the glimpse of Phin's lean, muscled body.

I didn't sigh, of course, but I did look, and even I had to admit—although not to Anne, of course—that it was a body worth sighing over if you were into that kind of thing.

But I certainly wasn't prepared to trek through the rainforest myself to see it at first hand.

'It sounds awful,' I told Phin. 'Hot and sweaty and crawling with insects…ugh.'

He leant forward, fixing me with that unnerving blue gaze. 'You say hot and sweaty, Summer,' he said, rocking his hand in an either/or gesture. 'I say heat and passion and excitement.'

Heat. Passion. Excitement. They were so not

me. But something about the words in Phin's mouth made me shift uneasily on the sofa. 'And what on earth makes you think I would like that?' I asked, with what I hoped was a quelling look.

'Your mouth.'

It was a bit like missing a step. I had the same lurch of the heart, punching the air from my lungs, the same hollowness in the stomach. My eyes were riveted to Phin's, and all at once their blueness was so intense that I felt quite dizzy with the effort of not tumbling into it.

'It just doesn't go with the rest of you,' he went on conversationally, while I was still opening and closing the mouth in question. 'You're all cool and crisp and buttoned up in your suit. But that mouth…' He put his head on one side and studied it. 'It makes me think there's more to you than that. It makes me think that you might have a secretly sensual side… Am I right?'

'Certainly not,' I blustered, unable to think of a suitably crushing reply. 'I can assure you that there isn't a single bit of me that wants to go to the rainforest.'

Phin clicked his tongue and shook his head sadly. 'Summer, Summer...I never thought you'd be a coward. Isn't it time you stepped out of your comfort zone and explored a different side of yourself?'

'I'm not into exploration,' I said coldly. 'That's the thing about comfort zones. They're comfortable. I've got no intention of making myself *un*comfortable if I don't have to.'

'But I'm afraid you *do* have to,' said Phin. 'You're on my team, and my team is going to Cameroon, whether you want to or not. So you'd better get used to the idea.'

I looked mutinously back at him. He was smiling, but there was an inflexibility to his jaw, a certain flintiness at the back of the blue eyes, that gave me pause and, like the coward Phin called me, I opted out of an argument just then.

I was sent off to liaise with Human Resources and find candidates for the first staff development trip. Phin said that he would organise everything at the Cameroonian end, but it would be my job to sort out flights, insurance, and all the other practicalities involved in taking a group of people overseas.

I didn't mind doing that as long as I didn't have to go myself. Still, he could hardly force me onto the plane, could he? I would be able to get out of it somehow, I reassured myself, and in the meantime I was much more excited about organising the *Glitz* interview. This was the chance I had dreamed about. At last I had a real reason to be in touch with Jonathan again.

Putting Africa out of my mind, I sat down to compose an e-mail to him. My heart was beating wildly at the mere thought of seeing him again, and I didn't trust my voice on the phone.

All I had to do was suggest that we meet the next day to discuss the *Glitz* feature, but you wouldn't believe how long it took me to produce a couple of lines that struck just the right balance between friendliness and cool professionalism.

I knew Jonathan would want to get involved. *Glitz* was stacked at every supermarket checkout in the land, and a positive piece about Phin taking up a new role at Gibson & Grieve would be fantastic publicity for us. Jonathan wouldn't let a PR opportunity like this go past without making sure Phin's office—i.e. me—was onboard.

Sure enough, he came back straight away.

Good idea. 12.30 tomorrow my office?
J

Not a long message, but I read it as carefully as the floweriest of love letters, desperate to decipher the subtext.

Good idea… That was encouraging, wasn't it? I mean, he could have just said *OK*, couldn't he? Or *fine*. So I chose to see some warmth there. Also, he'd signed it with an initial. That was an intimate kind of thing to do. Not as good as if he'd added a kiss, of course, but still better than a more formal *Jonathan*.

But the bit that really got my heart thumping with anticipation was the time. Twelve-thirty. Was it just the only time he could fit me in, or had he chosen it deliberately so that he could suggest lunch?

Naturally I spent the entire afternoon composing a suitable reply. The resulting masterpiece ran as follows: 12.30 tomorrow fine for me. See you then. S. And, yes, my finger did hover over the *x* key for a while before I decided on discretion. I didn't want to appear too pushy. Jonathan would hate that.

I discarded the idea of suggesting lunch myself for the same reason. But just in case Jonathan *was* thinking that we could discuss a PR strategy for Phin over an intimate lunch somewhere, I was determined to be prepared. Normally I'm very confident about putting outfits together, but I spent hours that night, dithering in front of my wardrobe, unable to decide what to wear the next day.

'What do you think?' I asked Anne.

I had dragged her away from yet another repeat of *Into the Wild*—wasn't there anything else on television?—so she wasn't best pleased. She sprawled grouchily on the bed.

'What I *think* is that you're wasting your time,' she said frankly. 'Face it, Summer, Jonathan's just not that into you. He's already made that crystal-clear.'

'He might change his mind,' I said, and even I could hear the edge of desperation in my voice.

'He won't,' said Anne, who had never liked Jonathan. 'Why can't you see it?' She sighed at my stubborn expression. 'For someone so clear-thinking, you're incredibly obtuse when it comes to Jonathan,' she told me. 'It's not like he ever made any effort for you, even when you were seeing each other. Why was he so keen to keep your affair a secret? It wasn't like either of you were involved with anyone else.'

'Jonathan didn't think it was appropriate to have a relationship in the office,' I said primly.

'You weren't *having* a relationship,' said Anne, exasperated. 'That was the whole point. You weren't even having much of an affair. You were just sleeping together when it suited Jonathan. If he'd been really keen on you he wouldn't have cared who knew. If he'd loved you he would have wanted to show you off, not hide you away as if he was ashamed of you.'

'Jonathan's not the kind of person who shows off,' I said, aware that I sounded defensive. 'I like that about him. He's sensible.'

'I think you're mad!' she said, throwing up her hands. 'I can't believe you spend every day with a hot guy like Phin Gibson and you're still obsessing about Jonathan Pugh!'

'Phin's not that hot,' I said, dismissing Anne's objections as I always did. 'And anyway, he's my boss. And we all know his idea of commitment is making it through to dessert without feeling trapped. I'm certainly not going to waste my time falling for him. That really would be mad! Now, concentrate, Anne. This is important. The twinset or the jacket?'

I held them on hangers in each hand. The cropped jacket was one of my favourites, a deep red with three-quarter-length sleeves, a shawl collar and a nipped-in waist. 'Too smart?' I asked dubiously. 'I don't want to look as if I'm trying too hard. But maybe the cardigan is a bit casual for the office?'

I'd bought the twinset with my Christmas bonus. A mixture of angora and cashmere, it was so beautifully soft I hadn't been able to resist it. I liked to take it out and stroke it, as if it were a kitten. To be honest, I wasn't sure that the colour—a dusty pink—was quite *me*, and I never felt entirely comfortable with the prettiness of it all, so I'd never worn it to the office. It was very different from my usual smartly tailored look, but perhaps different was what I needed.

Anne agreed. 'The twinset,' she said without hesitation. 'It's a much softer look for you, and if you leave your hair loose as well it'll practically scream *touch me, touch me*. Even Jonathan won't be able to miss the point.'

The hair was a step too far for me. If I turned up at work with my hair falling to my shoulders *everyone* would get the point. I might as well hang out a sign saying 'On the Pull'. So I tied my hair back as usual, but made up with extra care and painted my nails a pretty pink: Bubblegum—much nicer than it sounds. I wore the twinset, with a short grey skirt and heels just a little higher than usual.

Phin whistled when he came in—late, as usual—and saw me. 'You look very fetching, Summer,' he said. 'What's the occasion?'

'No occasion,' I said. 'I just felt like a change of image.'

'It's certainly that,' he said. 'You look very… touchable. How many people have stroked you to see if that cardigan is as soft as it looks?'

'A lot,' I said with a sigh. I'd lost count of the women who'd stroked my arm and ooh-ed and aah-ed over its softness. I couldn't blame them, really. Wearing it was like being cuddled by a kitten. 'It's a bit disconcerting to have perfect strangers running their hands down your arm.'

'But you can understand why they do,' said Phin. 'In fact, I'm sorry, but I'm just going to have to do it myself. I don't count as a perfect stranger, do I?' Without waiting for my reply, he smoothed his own hand down from my shoulder to my elbow, and I felt it through the fine wool like a brand. 'Incredibly soft,' he said, 'and very unexpected.'

Funny—I'd never felt anyone else's stroke quite like that. My skin was tingling where his fingers had touched me. I swallowed.

'I think I'll go back to a suit tomorrow.'

'That would be a shame,' said Phin. 'I like this new look a lot.'

Now all I needed was for Jonathan to like it, too. If the cardigan had the same effect on him, it would be worth feeling self-conscious now.

For the first time I realised that Phin didn't look quite his normal self either that morning. There was a distinctly frazzled air about him, and his shirt was even more crumpled than usual. Probably partying all night again with Jewel, I thought unsympathetically.

I was sure of it when he suggested having coffee immediately. 'In keeping with today's theme, I've bought Danish pastries for a change,' he said. 'I'm badly in need of some sugar!'

'Hangover?' I asked sweetly.

'Just a very fraught morning,' said Phin with a humorous look. 'I never thought I'd be glad to say I had to go to the office!'

He didn't say any more, and I didn't ask. I was too busy checking the clock every couple of minutes and willing the hands to move faster.

I decided that if Jonathan didn't suggest lunch, I would. I would make it very casual. *Do you want to grab a sandwich while we're talking?* Something like that.

I mouthed the words as my fingers rattled over the keyboard. The trouble was that I didn't do casual very well. Look how astounded everyone was when I appeared in a cardigan.

I knew the words would come out sounding stiff and awkward if I didn't get it right, but how was I supposed to practise when Phin was in and out of my office every five minutes, asking how to send a fax from his computer, wanting to borrow my stapler, giving me the dates for the Cameroon trip—about which I was still trying to keep a *very* low profile.

'You know, you could just buzz me and I'd come in to you,' I said, exasperated, in the end.

'I'd rather come out,' said Phin, picking up a couple of spare ink cartridges from my desk and attempting to juggle them. 'I feel trapped if I have to sit down for too long.'

I detoured back from the photocopier to snatch the cartridges out of the air. I put them in a desk drawer and shut it firmly as I sat down.

'Why don't you go for a walk?' I suggested through clenched teeth.

'It's funny you should say that. My producer just e-mailed me to say that we're going back to finish filming in Peru next week, so I'll be doing the last part of the trek again. I'll be away about twelve days.' Now he had my stapler in his hand, and was holding it out to me like a microphone. 'Do you think you'll miss me?'

'Frankly, no,' I said, taking the stapler from him and setting it back on the desk with a click. I glanced at the clock. Just past midday! I didn't have long. 'Are you going out for lunch?' I asked hopefully.

'I haven't got any plans,' said Phin. 'I might just—'

That was when my mother rang. As if I didn't have enough to cope with that morning!

'I just *had* to tell you,' she said excitedly. 'A new galactic portal is opening today!'

I love my mother, but sometimes I do wonder how we can possibly be related. I'd suspect a mix-up in the hospital if I hadn't been born into a commune, with who knows how many people dancing and chanting and shaking bells around my mother. It must have been the most godawful racket, and if had been me I would have told them all to go away and leave me to give birth in peace. But of course Mum—or Starlight, as she prefers to be called nowadays—was in her element. The wackier the situation, the more she loves it.

I pinched the bridge of my nose between thumb and forefinger. I knew better than to ask what a galactic portal was.

'That's great, Mum,' I said. 'Look, I can't really talk now—'

But she was already telling me about some ceremony she had taken part in the night before, that apparently involved much channelling of angels and merging of heart chakras.

'Such a beautiful spiritual experience!' she

sighed. 'So empowering! The energy vibrations now are quite extraordinary. Can't you *feel* them?'

I resisted the urge to bang my head against my desk.

'Er, no—no, I can't just this moment,' I said, aware that Phin was eavesdropping. I couldn't imagine him caring about the fact that this was obviously a personal phone call, but I hoped he couldn't hear anyway. My mother was deadly serious but, let's face it, she could sound nuts.

'That's because you're not open to the energy, darling,' my mother told me reproachfully. 'Have you been entering the crystal the way I showed you? You must let the love flow through your chakras.'

'Yes, yes, I will,' I said, one eye on the clock. After dragging all morning, it was suddenly whizzing round. If I wasn't careful, I'd be late for Jonathan. 'The thing is, Mum, I'm actually quite busy right now. Can I call you later?'

I'd finally managed to give her a mobile phone, which I paid for by direct debit. I knew she would never keep it topped up herself. My mother preferred spiritual forms of communication to the humdrum practicalities of paying phone bills or keeping track of credit.

'That would be lovely, darling, but I'll be seeing you soon,' she said. 'I'm coming to London, so we can talk properly then.'

Another time I would have been alarmed at her casual mention of a London visit, but I was desperate to get her off the phone before my meeting with Jonathan.

'That's great,' I said instead. 'Bye, then, Mum.'

I caught Phin's eye as I put the phone down. 'That was my mother,' I said unnecessarily.

'Is everything OK?'

'Oh, yes, fine,' I said airily. 'A new galactic portal is opening. You know how it is.'

'Blimey.' Phin sounded impressed. 'Is that good or bad?'

'I've no idea. Whatever it is, it seems to be keeping my mother busy.' I glanced at the clock again. Twelve-fourteen. I should think about getting ready.

I gathered my papers into a file and stood up. Only sixteen minutes and I'd be alone with Jonathan for the first time in weeks. I couldn't wait.

Edging round the desk, I opened my mouth to tell Phin that I was going to a meeting, but before I could make my escape I saw consternation on his face as he looked over my shoulder. I turned to see Jewel Stevens framed in the doorway.

To say that she came in wouldn't do her justice. You could tell that she was an actress. I felt that there should have been a fanfare—or possibly the theme tune from *Jaws*—as she waited until all eyes were on her before making her entrance.

'Hi, baby,' she cooed, her sultry brown eyes on Phin. I was fairly sure that she hadn't registered my existence.

'Jewel!' The appalled expression I had glimpsed had vanished, and he was once more Mr Charm. 'What are you doing here?'

She pouted at him, sweeping a glance up from under impossibly long lashes. 'I just wanted to make sure you weren't too cross with me after this morning.'

'No, no,' said Phin easily. 'I never liked that dinner service anyway.'

Jewel laughed, delighted at her own power, and then her voice dropped seductively. 'I came to make it up to you. To see if you missed me after last night.'

You had to hand it to her. Completely ignoring my presence, she wound her arms around his neck and kissed him on the mouth. And I don't mean a casual peck. I mean a full-on passionate kiss with tongues—well, I assume with tongues. It certainly looked that kind of kiss.

Anyway, by the time she had finished she was plastered all over him and twirling her tongue in his ear. Yuck. I can't bear anyone touching my ears—I'm funny like that—and it made me queasy just looking at her. Just as well I hadn't had my lunch yet.

I averted my gaze. No wonder Phin was looking tired this morning!

'What say we go back to my place?' Jewel was saying huskily. 'We can spend the afternoon together. Just wait until you see what I've got for you, tiger,' she whispered suggestively in his ear, and then—and I swear I'm not making this up—she growled.

Oh, please. I rolled my eyes mentally, only to catch Phin's gaze over her shoulder. He grimaced at me and mouthed an unmistakable *Help!*

I was half tempted to leave him to it, but there was such naked appeal in his eyes that I relented. 'You haven't forgotten your twelve-thirty meeting, have you?' I asked clearly.

'God, yes, I have!' Phin sent me a grateful look as he disentangled himself from her—which took some doing, I can tell you. Managing to free a hand, he slapped his head. 'I'm sorry, Jewel. I can't.'

Jewel's beautiful face darkened. 'Do you have to go? Meetings aren't important. What's it about?'

Another agonised look at me. 'You need to discuss PR strategy,' I supplied obediently.

'Yes, that's right. PR. So I'm afraid it *is* important.' Phin spread his hands disarmingly.

'Then I'll wait for you in your office.' She was twining herself around him again. Honestly, the woman was like an octopus. Phin would just manage to prise one of her hands away and the other would already be sliding round him.

'I think you'd get very bored, Jewel,' he said. 'It's likely to be a long meeting. We're going out to lunch. In fact, we'd better go—hadn't we, Summer?'

I looked at the clock. 'Definitely,' I said,

picking up the file. I didn't care what he did with Jewel, but I was meeting Jonathan at twelve-thirty if it killed me.

Jewel's beautiful sullen mouth was turned down. 'When will you be finished?'

'I'm not entirely sure,' said Phin, steering her towards the door. 'I'll give you a ring, OK?'

Still pouting, Jewel insisted on another kiss before she would let him go. 'See you later then, tiger.' She smirked, and sashayed off towards the lifts.

There was silence in the office. I looked at Phin. 'Tiger?'

He had the grace to squirm. 'Believe me, Jewel's the tiger. I'm the baby antelope here.'

'I'm sure you fought madly.'

'If I'd known what I was getting into I would have done,' he said frankly. 'I mean, she's gorgeous, and I've got to admit I was flattered when she made a beeline for me, but she gives a whole new meaning to high-maintenance. Talk about a prima donna! I must have withdrawn my attention for about ten seconds this morning, while I made myself some toast, and my eardrums are still ringing! She was throwing plates at the walls—it was like Greek night down at the local kebab shop. I'm buying plastic ones next time. I never thought I'd say it, but it was a real relief to come into the office and find you as cool and calm as ever.'

I certainly hadn't been feeling cool and calm, I thought, but could only be glad my fluttery nerves hadn't shown.

'Anyway, I owe you one,' he said. 'If you hadn't rescued me I'd have been dragged back to her lair and spat out later, an empty husk of a man.'

'Call it quits for the doughnuts,' I said. I looked at my watch and my heart gave a lurch. Twelve twenty-five. 'I'd better go.'

Phin peered round the doorway to check if Jewel was still waiting for the lift. Apparently she was, because he withdrew his head hastily. 'I might as well come, too,' he said.

I looked at him in dismay. I didn't want him muscling in on my *tête-à-tête* with Jonathan! 'I don't think you'll find it very interesting,' I tried, but Phin was already hustling me down the corridor away from the lifts.

'We'll take the stairs,' he muttered. 'Isn't your

meeting about PR, anyway?' he went on once safely out of Jewel's sight. 'I should know what's going on.'

'I'll fill you in on the details afterwards,' I tried.

'No, I'd better come. I wouldn't put it past Jewel to come back and surprise me,' said Phin, with an exaggerated grimace of fear. 'And where would I be without you to rescue me?'

If I resisted any more, Phin would start wondering why I was so keen to be on my own with Jonathan, and that was the last thing I wanted. I could hardly refuse to take my own boss to a meeting, after all, but I was rigid with disappointment as we made our way up to Jonathan's office on the floor above.

Not that Phin seemed to notice. He was in high good humour, having escaped Jewel's clutches, and he breezed into Jonathan's office and completely took over the meeting. I had no need to bring out my line about grabbing a sandwich.

'Let's talk over lunch,' said Phin, and bore us off to a wine bar tucked away in a side street between Covent Garden and the Strand.

So much for my date with Jonathan. I walked

glumly beside Phin, listening to him setting out to charm Jonathan, who was obviously delighted at Phin's unexpected appearance. I was feeling pretty miserable, if you want the truth. I couldn't fool myself that there had been even a flash of disappointment from Jonathan because he wouldn't be meeting me alone.

Still, I found myself grabbing onto pathetic crumbs of comfort—like the way he arranged for me to sit next to him at the table. Later, of course, I realised it was so that he could sit face to face with Phin, on the other side, but at the time it was all I had to hang on to.

Not that it did me much good. I wanted to concentrate on Jonathan, but somehow I couldn't with Phin sitting across the table exuding such vitality that even after what had obviously been a heavy night with Jewel everyone else seemed to fade in comparison to him. Whenever I tried to slide a glance at Jonathan my eyes would snag instead on Phin's smile, or Phin's solid forearms, or his hands that fiddled maddeningly with the cutlery as he talked and gesticulated.

The two men couldn't have been more of a contrast. Jonathan was in a beautifully cut grey suit, which he wore with a blue shirt and dotted silk tie. Anne would have looked at him and said conventional and boring, but to me he was mature and professional. Unlike Phin, whose hair could have done with a cut and who was wearing a casual shirt and chinos in neutral colours and yet still managed to look six times as colourful as anyone else in the room.

'*Glitz* are planning a major spread,' Jonathan was explaining to Phin. 'It's a great opportunity for us to promote a more accessible image. Market research shows that Gibson & Grieve are still seen as elitist, so for the new stores we need to present ourselves as ordinary and family-friendly. Your image as a celebrity will be very valuable to us, but up to now you've been associated with the wild. What we want is to associate you with the home, and we'd like *Glitz* to interview you at your house, so that their readers get an idea of you in a domestic setting.'

Jonathan paused delicately. 'If you have a girl-friend, it would be very good to get her involved as well—perhaps even give the impression that you're thinking of settling down. I did hear that you're going out with Jewel Stevens…?' He trailed off, more than a touch of envy in his tone.

Phin's eyes met mine. 'I'm not involving Jewel,' he said with a grin. 'It might give her all the wrong ideas—and besides, I wouldn't have any crockery left by the time *Glitz* turned up. I'm reduced to eating off paper plates as it is!'

'She sounds very feisty,' said Jonathan. I don't know if he was aiming for a man-about-town air or humour, but either way it didn't quite work.

I glanced at Phin and away again.

'Feisty is one way of putting it,' he said. 'Sorry, Jonathan, but I'm going to have to do this as single guy.'

Jonathan looked disappointed. I got the feeling that he would have liked to have talked more about Jewel. 'Well, perhaps you could give the impression that you're thinking of settling down without mentioning any names,' he suggested.

'I'll do my best.'

'What about your house? Do we need to redecorate for you?'

'Redecorate? I thought the article was supposed to be showing me as I am at home?'

'No, it's to show you at the kind of home we

want readers to associate with Gibson & Grieve,' Jonathan corrected him. He turned to me. 'Summer, you'd better check it out. You'll know what needs to be done.'

'She'll just tidy me up,' Phin protested.

'Summer's very competent,' said Jonathan.

Competent. You know, when you dream of what the man of your dreams will say about you, you think about words like *beautiful, amazing, sexy, passionate, incredible*. You never long for him to tell you're competent, do you?

'No redecorating,' said Phin firmly. 'If you make it all stylish it'll look and seem false, and that would do our image more harm than good. Summer can come and keep me on the straight and narrow in the interview, but I'm not changing the house. If you want readers to see what my home is like, we can show them. It's not as if I live in squalor.'

My only hope was that Phin might leave us after lunch, but, no, he insisted on walking back with us. So I never had one moment alone with Jonathan. I had to say goodbye to him in the lift as Phin and I got out on the floor below.

And that was my big date that I'd looked

forward to so much. A complete waste of make-up. Jonathan hadn't even commented on my cardigan.

Phin looked nervously around the office when we got back. 'She's gone—phew!' He wiped his brow in mock relief. 'Thanks again for earlier, Summer. It's good to know you can lie when you need to! If Jewel comes in again, I'm not here, OK?'

I was too cross about Jonathan to be tactful. I was even beginning to feel some sympathy for Jewel. At least she had the gumption to go for what she wanted. Jonathan evidently found her feistiness appealing. Perhaps I should have tried smashing a few plates.

'If you don't want to see her again, you should tell her yourself…tiger,' I said sharply, and Phin winced.

'I'll try,' he said. 'But Jewel isn't someone who listens to what she doesn't want to hear. Still, I'm going away in a few days,' he remembered cheerfully. 'She'll soon lose interest if I'm not around.'

CHAPTER FOUR

HE LEFT for Peru a week later. 'How long will you be away?' I asked him.

'We should be able to wrap it up in twelve days.' Phin looked up from the computer screen with a grin. 'Why? Do you think you'll miss me after all?'

'No,' I said crushingly. 'I just need to know when to arrange a date with *Glitz*.'

But the funny thing was that I *did* miss him a bit. I realised I'd got used to him being in the office, managing to seem both lazy and energetic at the same time, and without him everything seemed strangely flat.

I told myself that I enjoyed the peace and quiet, and that it was a relief to be able to get on with some work without being teased or constantly interrupted by frivolous questions or made to stop and eat doughnuts—OK, I didn't mind that bit *so* much. I had a whole week without Phin juggling with my stapler and my sticky note dispenser, or messing around with the layout of my desk, which I know quite well he only did to annoy.

He was always picking things up and then putting them down in the wrong place, or at an odd angle, and he seemed to derive endless amusement from watching me straighten them. Sometimes I'd try and ignore it, but it was like trying to ignore an itch. After a while my hand would creep out to rearrange whatever it was he had dislodged, at which point Phin would shout, 'Aha! I knew you couldn't do it!'

I mean, what kind of boss carries on like that? It was deeply unprofessional, as I was always pointing out, but that only made Phin laugh harder.

So all in all I was looking forward to having the office to myself for a few days, but the moment he'd gone I didn't quite know what to do with myself.

That first morning on my own I went down to the kitchen to make myself some coffee. I'd got out of the habit of buying myself a doughnut, I realised. Phin always bought them now, and I'd forgotten that I wouldn't have anything to have with my coffee. It wouldn't kill me, but the lack of sugar just added to my grouchiness as I carried my mug back to my desk.

Khalid from the postroom was just on his way out of my office. 'I've left the mail on your desk,' he told me. 'You've got a Special Delivery, too.'

I'd ordered a scanner the day before. The supplies department must have moved quickly for once, I thought, but as I set down my mug I saw a small confectionery box sitting in front of my keyboard. 'Summer Curtis, Monday' was scribbled on the top. Not a scanner, then.

Puzzled, I opened it up. Inside, sitting on a paper napkin, was a doughnut.

There was a business card, too. I pulled it out. It had Phin's name and contact details on one side. On the other he had scrawled, 'I didn't want to think of you without your sugar fix. P x'

My throat felt ridiculously tight. Nobody had ever done anything as thoughtful for me before.

Of course it didn't mean anything, I was quick to remind myself. It was just part of Phin's pathological need to make everyone like him. His charm was relentless.

But still I found myself—annoyingly—thinking about him, about where he was and what he was doing, and when I picked up the phone and heard his voice my heart gave the most ridiculous lurch.

'Just thought I'd check in,' said Phin. 'I hardly know what to do with myself. I'm so used to you telling me what to do and where to be all day. I've got used to being organised. Are you missing me yet?'

'No,' I lied, because I knew he'd be disappointed if I didn't. 'But thank you for the doughnut. How on earth did you organise it?'

'Oh, that was easy. I had a word with Lucia—who, by the way, smiled at me the other day, so you're not the only favourite now—and I asked her to send you a selection, so that you get something different every day I'm away. I think we're in a doughnut rut.'

'I like my rut,' I said, but I might as well have spared my breath. Phin was determined that I would try something different.

Sure enough, the next day an apricot Danish

arrived at half past ten, and even though I was determined not to like it as much as a doughnut, I had to admit that it was delicious.

The next day brought an almond croissant, and the one after that an apple strudel, and then an éclair. Pastries I'd never seen before appeared on my desk, and I found myself starting to glance at the clock after ten and wondering what I'd have with my coffee that day. I'd try and guess what would be in the box— vanilla turnover? *Pain au chocolat?*—but I never got it right.

Inevitably word got round about my special deliveries. I wasn't the only one who was guessing. I heard afterwards they were even taking bets on it in Finance.

'I wish my boss would send me pastries,' my friend Helen grumbled. 'You'd think in Food Technology it would be a perk of the job. You are lucky. Phin's so lovely, isn't he?'

I heard that a lot, and although I always said that he was a nightmare to work for, the truth was that I was finding it hard to remember just how irritating he was. When he walked into the office the following Tuesday, my heart jumped into my throat and for one panicky moment I actually forgot how to breathe.

He strolled in, looking brown and fit, his eyes bluer than ever, and instantly the air was charged with a kind of electricity. Suddenly I was sharply aware of everything: of colour of my nails flickering over the keyboard—Cherry Ripe, if you're interested—of the computer's hum, of the feel of the glasses on my nose, the light outside the window. It was as if the whole office had snapped into high definition.

'Good morning,' I said, and Phin peered at me in surprise.

'Good God, what was that?'

'What was what?' I asked, thrown.

'No, no…it's OK. For a moment there I thought I saw a smile.'

'I've smiled before,' I protested.

'Not like that. It was worth coming home for!' Phin came to sit on the edge of my desk and picked up the stapler. 'I'm not going to ask if you missed me because you'll just look at me over your glasses and say no.'

'I would have said a bit—until you started fiddling,' I said, removing the stapler from his grasp and setting it back into its place. 'But now I've remembered how irritating you are.'

Deliberately, Phin reached out and pushed the stapler out of alignment with one finger. 'Irritating? Me?'

'Stop it,' I said, slapping his hand away. I straightened the stapler once more. 'Haven't you got some other trip to go on? I'm sure they must need you in Ulan Bator or Timbuktu or somewhere.'

'Nope. Next time you're coming with me.' He had started on the scissors now, snapping them at me as he talked. 'So, what's the news here?'

'We've set up your *Glitz* interview for Thursday,' I told him. 'The interviewer is called Imelda Ross, and she's bringing a photographer with her. They'll be at your house at ten, so can you please make sure you're ready for them?'

'That's an appointment, not news,' he said. 'What's the gossip? Has Lex run off with a lap dancer? Has Kevin been caught siphoning funds to some offshore bank account?' Kevin was our Chief Financial Officer and famously prudent.

'Nothing so exciting, I'm afraid. Everyone's been doing what they always do.'

Actually, that wasn't *quite* true. Jonathan was looking much more relaxed these days. I had shared a lift with him a few days earlier, and instead of being stiff and awkward he had smiled and chatted about the spell of fine weather.

I'd replayed the conversation endlessly, of course, and was hugging the hope that he might be warming to me again. Between that and Phin's pastries I'd been happier than I'd been for ages—but I didn't think that would be of much interest to Phin, even if I had been prepared to confess it, which I wasn't.

'According to the gossip mags, Jewel Stevens has got a new man,' I offered instead.

'*Has* she? Excellent! I was hoping she'd lost interest.'

'She rang looking for you a couple of times, but I didn't think you'd want to speak to her in Peru, so I said you were out of contact.'

'Summer, you're a treasure,' he told me, putting down the scissors at last and digging around at his feet. 'So, even though you haven't missed me, you deserve a reward,' he said as he produced a paper bag. 'I've brought us something special to celebrate my return.'

The 'something special' turned out to be a cream doughnut each. 'I didn't feel we knew each other well enough to tackle one of these before,' he said as I eyed it dubiously, wondering how on earth I was going to eat it elegantly.

'I defy you to eat one of these without making a mess,' Phin added, reading my expression without any difficulty.

I couldn't, of course. I started off taking tiny nibbles, until he couldn't bear it any more.

'Get on with it, woman,' he ordered. 'Stop messing around at the edges. Take a good bite and enjoy it! That's not a bad recipe for life, now I come to think of it,' he said, watching as I sank my teeth obediently into the middle of the doughnut and cream spurted everywhere. 'The doughnut approach to living well. I might write a book about it.'

'Make sure you include a section on how to clean up all the mess,' I said, dabbing at my mouth with my fingers, torn between embarrassment and laughter. I spotted a blob of cream on my skirt. 'Ugh, I've got cream *everywhere*!'

'The best things in life are messy,' said Phin.

'Not as far as I'm concerned,' I said, as I carefully wiped the cream from my skirt. 'But maybe I'll make an exception for cream dough-nuts. It was delicious!'

With a final lick of my fingers, I got to my feet. 'I'd better get back to work,' I said.

Phin got up, too. His smile had faded as he watched me eat the doughnut, and his expression was oddly unreadable for once. He was looking at me so intently that I hesitated.

'What?' I asked.

'You've missed a bit,' he said and, reaching out, he wiped a smear of cream from my cheek, just near my mouth. Then he offered me his finger to lick.

I stared at it, mesmerised by the vividness with which I could imagine my tongue against his finger. I could practically taste the sweet-ness of the cream, feel the contrast between its smoothness and the firmness of his skin, and a wave of heat pulsed up from my toes to my cheeks and simmered in my brain. For one awful moment I was afraid that the top of my head would actually blow off.

Horrified by how intimate the mere idea seemed, and about Phin—my boss!—of all people, I found myself taking a step back and shaking my head at the temptation.

Phin's eyes never left my mouth as he licked the cream off himself.

'Yum, yum,' he said softly.

I know, it doesn't sound very erotic, but my heart was thudding so loudly I was sure he must hear it. My pulse roared in my ears and I had a terrible feeling that I might literally be steaming. I had to get out of the room before Phin noticed.

I cleared my throat with an effort. 'I…er…I should let you get on. Haven't you got a meeting now?'

'I have?'

'Yes, in HR. You wanted me to set it up for you, to talk to Jane about staff development and the Cameroon trip. It's in the diary.' I could feel myself babbling as I backed away towards the door. 'I'll forward the e-mail to you…'

Somehow I made it back to my desk, and had to spend a few minutes just breathing very carefully.

I felt very odd, almost shaken. I had never thought about Phin that way before. I had never thought about Jonathan like that either, to be honest. I loved Jonathan, but he was safe. This wild pounding of my blood felt dark and rude and dangerous, and I didn't like it.

I pulled myself together at last. A momentary aberration, I told myself. A huge fuss about nothing. I mean, we hadn't even touched. A flick of Phin's finger against my cheek. That was all that had happened. Nothing at all, in fact.

I was just…hot. Was this what a hot flush was like? I wondered wildly. If so, I wasn't looking forward to the menopause at all.

Jittery and unsettled, I took myself off to the Ladies' to run cold water over my wrists. Someone had once told me that was the best way to cool yourself down, and I had no intention of splashing cold water all over my make-up. I wasn't in *that* much of a state.

I met Lex's PA, Monique, on her way in at the same time. Typical, isn't it, that the moment you're desperate to be alone people you don't normally see for ages start popping out of the woodwork? This wasn't even Monique's floor.

I was afraid that she would comment on how hot and flustered I looked, but fortunately she didn't seem to notice anything amiss. Reassured, I stopped to chat.

See, I told myself, all I needed was a little normality. It was a relief to talk about ordinary stuff, and I began to feel myself again.

'So what's the gossip?' I asked Monique, remembering Phin's question earlier. Monique was famously discreet, but if she did have any news it would be good to be able to pass a titbit on to Phin. At least it would be something to say other than *Could we try that cream on the finger thing again?*

'Funny you should say that.' Monique glanced around and lowered her voice, even though there was no one else in there with us. 'Have you seen Jonathan recently?'

Phin and the cream were instantly forgotten. 'A couple of times,' I said, as casually as I could. My poor old heart was working overtime this morning. Now it was pattering away at the mention of Jonathan. 'Why?'

'He's a changed man, isn't he?'

I thought of how relaxed he had looked the last time I'd seen him. 'He seems to be in a good mood.'

'Yes, and we all know why now!'

'We do?' I asked cautiously.

Monique grinned. 'Our steady, sensible Jonathan is in love.'

Not content with pattering, my heart pole-vaulted into my throat, where it lodged, hammering wildly. 'In love?' I croaked.

She nodded. 'And with Lori, of all people! I wouldn't have thought she was his type at all, but they're all over each other and they're not even bothering to try and hide it. Oh, well, at least he's happy.' She looked at her watch. 'I'd better get on. Lex will be wondering what's happened to me.'

There was a rushing in my ears. I think I must have said something, but I've no idea what, and Monique waggled her fingers in farewell as she hurried off, oblivious to the fact that my world had come crashing down around me.

Shaking, feeling sick, I shut myself in a cubicle and put my head between my knees. *I mustn't cry, I mustn't cry, I mustn't cry,* I told myself savagely. I had the rest of the afternoon to get through, and if I cried my mascara would run and everyone would know my heart was broken.

I don't know how long I sat there, but it can't have been that long. I knew I had to get back.

Lifting my head, I drew long, painful breaths to steady myself. I could do this.

Thank God for make-up. I reapplied lipstick very carefully and studied my expression. My eyes held a stark expression, but you'd have had to know me very well to spot that anything was wrong. Inside I felt ragged and raw, and I walked stiffly, so as not to jar anything, but outwardly I was perfectly composed.

I made it back to my desk and sank down in my chair, staring blankly at the computer screen. I just had to sit there for another few hours and then I'd be able to go home. Phin had gone out to his lunch with Jane, the director of HR, so I was spared him at least. Those blue eyes might be full of laughter but they didn't miss much.

By the time he came back it was after four, and I had had plenty of time to compose myself. I ached all over with the effort of not falling apart, and my brain felt as if it had an elastic band snapped round it, but I was able to meet his gaze when he came in.

'How was your meeting?' I asked, knowing Phin would never guess what it cost me to sound normal.

'Very useful. Jane's great, isn't she? We talked about Cameroon and she's all for a trial visit to see—' He broke off and frowned. 'What's the matter?'

'Nothing.' My throat was so tight I had to force the word out.

'Don't try and deny it,' said Phin. 'That stapler is a millimetre out of alignment. And...' he peered closer '...yes, I do believe that's a chip in your nail polish!' The laughter faded from his voice and from his face. 'Come on, I can see in your eyes that something's wrong. What is it?'

'It's...nothing.' I couldn't look at him. I stared fiercely away, pressing my lips together in one straight line.

'You're not the kind of person that gets upset about nothing,' he said gently. Going back to the door, he closed it. 'Tell me,' he said.

There was a great, tangled knot of hurt in my throat. I knew if I even tried to say Jonathan's name I would break down completely, and I wasn't sure I could bear the humiliation. 'I...can't.'

'OK,' he said. 'You don't need to say anything. But we're going out. Get your coat.'

I was too tired and miserable to object. He

took me to a dimly lit bar, just beginning to fill with people leaving work early. Like us, I supposed. We found a table in a corner and Phin looked around for a waiter.

'What would you like?' he asked. 'A glass of wine?'

God, I was so predictable, I realised. No wonder Jonathan didn't want me. Even Phin could see that I was the kind of girl who sensibly just had a small glass of white wine before going home. I was boring.

'Actually, I'd like a cocktail,' I said with a shade of defiance.

'Sure,' said Phin. 'What kind?'

I picked up the menu on the table and scanned it. I would love to have been the kind of girl who could order Sex on a Beach or a Long Slow Screw Against a Wall without sounding stupid, but I wasn't. 'A pomegranate martini,' I decided, choosing one at random.

His mouth flickered, but he ordered it straight-faced from the waiter, along with a beer for himself.

When it came, it looked beautiful—a rosy pink colour with a long twirl of orange peel curling through it. I was beginning to regret my choice by then, but was relieved to take a sip and find it delicious. Just like fruit juice, really.

I was grateful to Phin for behaving quite normally. He chatted about his meeting with Jane, and I listened with half an ear as I sipped the martini which slipped down in no time. I even began to relax a bit.

'Another one?' Phin asked, beckoning the waiter over.

About to say that I shouldn't, I stopped myself. Sod it, I thought. I had nothing to go home for. 'Why not?' I said instead.

When the second martini arrived, I took another restorative pull through the straw and sat back. I was beginning to feel pleasantly fuzzy around the edges.

'Thank you,' I said on a long sigh. 'This was just what I needed.'

'Can you talk about it yet?'

Phin's voice was warm with sympathy. The funny thing was that it didn't feel at all awkward to be sitting there with him in the dim light. Maybe it was the martini, but all at once he felt like a friend, not my irritating boss. Only that morning the graze of his finger had reduced me to mush, but it was too bizarre to remember that now.

I sighed. 'Oh, it's just the usual thing.'

'Boyfriend trouble?'

'He's not my boyfriend any more. The truth is, he was never really my boyfriend at all,' I realised dully. 'But I loved him. I still do.'

In spite of myself, my eyes started to fill with tears. 'He told me before Christmas that he wanted out, that he didn't think it was working,' I went on, my voice beginning to wobble disastrously. 'I'd been hoping and hoping that he'd change his mind, and I let myself believe that he was beginning to miss me, but I just found out today that he's going out with Lori and he's mad about her and I don't think I can bear it.'

I couldn't stop the tears then. It was awful. I hate crying, hate that feeling of losing control, but there was nothing I could do about it.

Phin saw me frantically searching for tissue, and silently handed me a paper napkin that had come with the bowl of nuts.

'I'm sorry, I'm sorry,' I wept into it.

'Hey, don't be sorry. It sucks. Who is this guy,

anyway?' he said. 'Do you want me to go and kill him for you? Would that help?'

'I don't think Lex would be very pleased if you did.' I sniffed into the napkin. 'He'd have to find a new PR person.'

Phin's brows crawled up to his hairline. 'Are we talking about *Jonathan Pugh*?'

I could see him trying to picture Jonathan's appeal. I know Jonathan isn't the sexiest looking guy in the world, but it was about more than looks.

'Jonathan's everything I ever wanted,' I told him tearfully. 'He's a bit older than me, I know, but he's so steady, so reliable. He seems reserved, but I always had the feeling that he'd be different in private, and he is. I never thought I'd have a chance with him, but then there was the summer party…'

I'll never forget my starry-eyed amazement when Jonathan came over to talk to me, and suggested going for a quiet drink away from all the noise. I'd been bedazzled by all my dreams coming true at once.

'I was so happy just to be with him,' I told Phin. Now I'd started talking, it was as if I couldn't stop. I had to blurt it all out. I gulped at my martini. 'I'd never been in love before, not like that, and when I was with him it felt like I had everything I'd ever wanted. I didn't mind that he wanted to keep our relationship a secret—to me that was just him being sensible, and I loved him for that, too. But he's not being sensible with Lori,' I said bitterly. 'He's not keeping *her* a secret. He doesn't care who knows how he feels about her.'

My mouth began to tremble wildly again. 'It wasn't that he didn't want to have a proper relationship. He just didn't want *me*. He wanted someone like Lori, who's pretty and feminine.'

'I bet she isn't prettier than you,' said Phin.

'She is. If you saw her, you'd know.'

I'd never liked Lori. She's the kind of woman who gives the impression of being frail and shy and helpless, but who always manages to get her own way. Men hang around, asking her if she's all right the whole time. As far as I knew Lori had no female friends—always a bad sign, in my opinion—but even I had to admit she was very pretty. She was tiny, with a tumble of blonde curls, huge blue eyes and a soft, breathy little voice.

Phin wouldn't be able to resist her any more than Jonathan had.

'OK, maybe she's pretty,' Phin allowed, 'but you're *beautiful*, Summer.'

'I'm not.' I blew my nose on the napkin. 'I'm ordinary. I know that.'

He laughed at that. 'You are so not ordinary, Summer! You've got fantastic bones and beautiful skin and your eyes are incredible. And don't get me started on your mouth… Your trouble is that you don't make the most of yourself.'

'I do,' I protested, still tearfully. 'Look at me.' I gestured down at my suit. Even in the depths of my misery I knew it was better not to draw attention to my face right then. I'm not a pretty crier. Maybe the likes of Lori can cry without their skin going blotchy and their eyes puffy and their nose running, but I couldn't. 'I always take trouble over my clothes,' I pointed out. 'I never go out without make-up. What more can I do?'

'You could let your hair down sometimes,' said Phin, lifting a hand as if to touch it, but changing his mind at the last minute. 'It looks as if it would be beautiful, thick and silky. It would make you look more…' he searched for the right word '…accessible,' he decided in the end, and I remembered what Anne had said about changing my image by letting my hair hang loose.

But what difference would it have made? 'What's the point in looking accessible when I'm boring?' I asked despairingly. 'Jonathan still wouldn't want me.'

'He must have wanted you at some point or he wouldn't have got involved with you in first place.'

'No, he didn't.' I was just starting to accept the truth. 'I flung myself at him, and I must have been convenient, but he never meant it to be more than that. He didn't want *me*. And why should he? I'm boring and sensible and practical,' I raged miserably, remembering now—too late—some of the things Jonathan had said. In hindsight, it was all so obvious. Only I hadn't wanted to see the truth before.

'Jonathan doesn't want someone as competent as he is. He doesn't want someone who can look after herself. He wants someone needy and feminine—like Lori. Someone he can look after. But I can't do needy. I'm too used to dealing with everything, ever since I was child. I can't help it, but Jonathan thinks it makes me bossy. He used to make comments about it. I thought he was being affectionate, but now I wonder if it really bothered him. Funny how a man is never bossy, isn't it?' I added in a bitter aside. 'A man is always assertive or controlling, but never, ever bossy.'

'I don't think you're bossy,' said Phin. 'You're practical, which is a very different thing.'

'Jonathan thinks I am. He just got bored with me. All that time I was telling myself how much I loved him, he was losing interest. I should have realised that he hadn't invested anything in the relationship. He didn't even leave a toothbrush at my flat. When he ended it, there was nothing to discuss.'

Oh, dear, here came the tears again. I groped around for the wet napkin until Phin found me another, and I scrubbed furiously at my cheeks before drawing a shuddering breath.

'When Monique told me about Lori today, it just made me realise what a fool I've been about everything,' I said. 'I'd had this dream in my head for so long, and it was all wrapped up with being with Jonathan and feeling safe, but I should have known it was too good to be true,' I said wretchedly. 'He'd never want someone like me.'

'But you still want him?'

I nodded. 'I love him,' I said, my voice catching.

'Then I think you should go out and get him back,' said Phin. 'I didn't have you down as someone who would give up as easily as that. What have you been doing since you split up?'

'Nothing.'

'Precisely, and look where it's got you. You're miserable, and Jonathan's dating a woman named after a truck. Lori? I mean, how serious can he be?'

I looked at him. 'That's a pathetic joke,' I said, but I managed a watery smile even so.

'I'm just saying you shouldn't give up,' Phin said. 'Your trouble is that you're too subtle. I had lunch with you both the other day, and I didn't have a clue that there had been anything at all between you. I wouldn't be surprised if Jonathan thinks you don't care one way or the other. I suggest we have another drink,' he went on, gesturing for the waitress to bring another round, 'and plan your strategy.'

I considered that, my brow creased with the effort of thinking after two martinis. 'You think I should tell Jonathan how I feel?'

'Absolutely not!' Phin tutted. 'Really, Summer, you haven't got a clue, have you? If you get heavy on him he'll panic and think you're about to drag him off to the suburbs via the nearest registry office—which is what you want, of course, but this is not the time to tell him that. You've got to reel him in first.'

'Well, what do you suggest, if you're such an expert?' I asked, wiping mascara away with the napkin. What was the point of waterproof mascara if you couldn't cry? I would have to write and complain. 'If I tell him how I feel, I'm too intense. If I don't, he won't notice because I'm so boring and predictable.' I lapsed back into gloom once more.

Another beer and a fresh martini were placed on the table. Phin pushed my glass towards me. 'For a start, you've got to get this idea that you're boring out of your head,' he told me sternly. 'You're smart, you're funny—not always deliberately, I'll grant you—and you're sexy as hell.'

CHAPTER FIVE

I STARED at him. *Sexy?* I was sensible, practical, reliable. Not sexy.

Jewel was sexy, pressing herself against him and sticking her tongue in his ear. Not me, with my glasses on a chain and my neat suits. Phin was either being kind or making fun of me.

For a fleeting moment I remembered the way I had felt as he'd wiped that blob of cream from my cheek, but then I pushed the memory aside. It was too incongruous.

'All you've got to do is make Jonathan appreciate what an incredible woman you are,' said Phin.

Yeah, right. 'How?' I asked, with a trace of sullenness. 'He never appreciated how "incredible" I was before.'

'Make him jealous,' said Phin promptly. 'I know guys like Jonathan. Hell, I *am* a guy like Jonathan, and if I saw you with another man I'd be intrigued at the very least. I guarantee Jonathan would start to remember what he saw in you if there's another guy sniffing around and making it obvious that he thinks you're incredible.'

'Well, yes, brilliant idea,' I said, picking up my glass. The third martini was definitely kicking in now. 'There's just one problem. I don't have another guy.'

'Start dating again,' said Phin, as if it was obvious.

'Oh, sure,' I said sarcastically. The martinis had made me bolshy, but it was better than snivelling. 'That's easy. I'll just snap my fingers and produce a man.' I patted my pockets. 'I'm sure I left one or two lying around somewhere…'

Phin looked at me appreciatively. 'I see you're feeling better,' he said. 'Look, it can't be that hard for a girl who looks like you to find a guy. Go and stand at the bar and smile, and I bet they'll be falling over themselves. Better still, eat a cream doughnut.'

There was a tiny silence. I flickered a glance at Phin. He was smiling, but the blue eyes held that odd expression again—the one that made me feel as if the world was tilting out of kilter.

'You have no idea, do you?' he said.

I swallowed. I didn't want to remember that disconcerting wave of heat. I didn't want to think about what it meant.

'I don't think it would be that easy,' I told him, my eyes sliding away from his. 'And even if I *did* find a boyfriend who wouldn't mind the fact that I don't actually want to be with him, when would Jonathan ever find out?'

'I see what you mean. Someone at work would be better.'

'Except if it was someone at work Jonathan would just feel sorry for him.' My confidence was crumbling again. Quick, it was time for another gulp of pomegranate martini.

'Not if it was obvious he was mad about you.'

'Oh, so now I have to find a boyfriend who can act, too? I'd have to hire him, and where do you suggest I look?'

'What about right here?'

I looked around the bar. 'How do I know if any of these guys can act? Well, the barmen are probably resting actors, but I'd never dare talk to them—they're far too cool.'

'No, *here*,' said Phin, tapping his chest.

My jaw dropped. *'You?'*

'There's no need to look like that! I'm perfect.'

'I know you think so,' said the third martini, and Phin grinned.

'I do think so, and so will you if you think about it,' he said. 'Jonathan can hardly not notice if you're with me, and I think you'll find I'm not a bad actor. They still talk about my Ugly Sister in the school pantomime and, according to my mother, I stole the show in the nativity play as the sheep that fell over when it tried to kneel in front of the manger.'

'I don't know why you're not in line for an Oscar,' I said, 'but why would you want to squander your great talent on me?'

'I like you,' said Phin simply, 'even if you are a bit sharp with me sometimes. If I can help you, I will. Besides, it might work out quite well for me from a PR point of view.'

I frowned. 'How do you work that out?'

'Think about it. Jonathan was very keen to push my family credentials in the *Glitz* interview. How better to do that than pretend I'm about to settle down with you? You can hang around and look good for the article, which means that even if Jonathan hasn't got the idea before, he definitely will then. A double whammy.'

He sat back smugly while I sipped my martini and considered what he had said. Surely it couldn't be as easy as Phin seemed to believe?

'What about Jewel?' I prevaricated.

'What about her? You said yourself that she's been going out with someone else, poor guy. I'm well out of that one!' said Phin. 'I wouldn't have had a plate left in the house. But now I come to think of it,' he went on, 'it might not be a bad idea to let her see I'm unavailable now. Just in case she's thinking she might pick up where we left off before I went to Peru.'

'I can't believe you'd have much trouble finding someone else to make sure she gets the point,' I demurred. 'There must be much more likely types who would give the impression that you're ready to settle down.'

'I wouldn't want to give anyone the wrong idea,' said Phin, not bothering to deny it. It would have been annoying if he had, but I was annoyed anyway. 'I'm not the settling down kind,' he said. 'At least with you we'd both know it was just a pretence.'

I blame it on the pomegranate martinis, but it was starting to make a weird kind of sense.

'No one would believe that I was really your girlfriend,' I said. 'You're used to going out with actresses and models.'

'Which is why they'll think I'm serious if they see me with you.'

My, this was doing wonders for my ego.

'It would only be for a few weeks,' Phin was saying. 'You wouldn't have to do much. Just be seen out at a few parties with me and hang around looking like a girlfriend for the interview. Then we can seem to break it off later, so I can carry on avoiding commitment while you walk off into the sunset with Jonathan.'

'Do you really think it would make a difference with Jonathan?' I asked wistfully.

'Listen, do you really want him back or not?'

'I really do.'

'Even though he's made you feel boring and unlovable?'

'I love him,' I said, dangerously close to getting weepy again.

'OK,' said Phin, 'if Jonathan is what you really want, then I think you deserve what you want. The first thing is to make him realise that you're not boring at all, that you're quite capable of being spontaneous when you've got the right incentive. Make him think that it's *his* fault you never had much fun with him—which it probably is, by the way. We're going to convince him that we're having a raging affair, and he's sure to sit up and take notice.'

'How do we go about having an affair?' I said doubtfully. I couldn't see myself being convincing as someone in the throes of a raging affair somehow. It wasn't the kind of thing I would do. It wasn't the kind of thing I liked, to be honest. It smacked too much of losing control and abandoning yourself. I liked things calm and steady and *safe*.

'Well, let's see,' said Phin with a grin. 'I could take you back to my place. We'll say it's just for a drink, but we won't be able to keep our hands off each other. The moment we're through the front door I'll start kissing you, and you'll kiss me back. You'll fall back against the door and pull me with you—'

'I don't mean really have an affair,' I interrupted, scarlet. I was horrified at how vividly I could imagine it, and there was a strange thumping deep inside me. Jonathan had never lost control like that. I was beginning to feel very odd, but I hoped very much that was down to the martinis. 'I meant…how would we make everyone believe it? We can hardly send round an e-mail announcement that we're sleeping together.'

Phin didn't seem to think that would be a problem. 'We'll go to a couple of parties, maybe leave work together—or even better arrive together—and word will get round in no time. If you can contrive to blush whenever my name is mentioned in the Ladies', or wherever you girls all congregate, so much the better. And remember how besotted I'm going to be with you,' he went on. 'I won't be able to keep my hands off you—especially when Jonathan is around. I don't think it will take long before he gets the point.'

I buried my nose in my martini, trying not to

wonder what it would be like to have Phin putting his arm around me, sliding his hand down my back. Would he twine his fingers around mine? Would he stroke my hair?

Would he *kiss* me?

The breath rushed out of my lungs at the thought. *Would* he? And if he did what would it be like?

My heart was thudding painfully—ba-*boom*, ba-*boom*, ba-*boom*—and I had to moisten my lips before I could speak. This was about Jonathan, remember?

'But if Jonathan thinks I'm with you, he'll assume I'm not interested in him any more,' I objected.

'Once he starts paying attention—and he will—you'll have to let him know that you just might be tempted away from me. If you can do it without seeming too keen. You might have to spend some time alone together...' Phin snapped his fingers. 'Of course! Jonathan can come to Cameroon. If you can't seduce him back on a steamy tropical night, Summer, I wash my hands of you!'

I thought about it as I sucked on the long curl of orange peel which was all that was left at the bottom of my glass. Apart from the reminder of Cameroon, which I'd been rather hoping he'd forgotten about, I was struggling to think of a good argument as to why Phin's idea wouldn't work.

The third martini wasn't helping. I was feeling distinctly fuzzy by now, and finding it hard to concentrate.

Phin followed my gaze to the empty glass. 'Had enough?' he asked, and I bridled at the humorous understanding in his voice.

A sensible girl would say yes at this point, but being sensible hadn't got me anywhere, had it?

'No,' I said clearly. Well, it was *meant* to sound clear. Whether it did is doubtful. 'I'd love another one.'

One of Phin's brows lifted. 'Are you sure?'

'Absho—ab*so*lutely sure.'

'It's your hangover,' he said, the corner of his mouth quirking in that lop-sided smile of his. He beckoned the waitress over. 'Another pomegranate martini for my little lush here, and I'll have another half.'

I waited until she had set the glasses on the table. Part of me knew quite well that Phin's plan was madness, but I hadn't been able to come up with a single argument to convince him how ridiculous the idea was.

'Do you really think it would work?' I asked, almost shyly.

'What's the worst that could happen if it doesn't?' Phin countered. 'You'd be in the same situation you are now, but at least you'll know you did everything you could to make your dream come true. That has to be better than just sitting and watching it disappear, doesn't it? And, if nothing else, we'll have promoted the family image of Gibson & Grieve with this interview. As a good company girl, I know you'll be glad to have done your bit!'

He was watching my face.

'It's a risk,' he said in a different voice, 'but you don't get what you really want without taking chances.'

I looked back at him, biting my lip.

'So,' he said, lifting his glass, 'do we have a deal?'

And I, God help me, chinked my glass against his. 'Deal,' I said.

* * *

'Good morning, Summer!' Phin's cheery greeting scraped across my thumping head.

'Not so loud,' I whispered, without even lifting my head from the desk, where I'd been resting it ever since I'd staggered into work twenty minutes earlier. Late, for the first time in my life. I would have been mortified if I had had any feelings to spare. As it was, I had to save my energy for basic survival. Breathing was about all I could manage right then, and even that hurt.

'Oh, dear, dear, dear.' I could picture him standing over me, blue eyes alight with laughter, lips pursed in mock reproach. 'Is it possible you're regretting that last martini?'

I groaned. 'Go away and leave me to die in peace!'

'Aren't you feeling well?' Phin enquired solicitously.

'How could you possibly have guessed that?' I mumbled, still afraid to move my head in case it fell off.

'I'm famed for my powers of deduction. The FBI are always calling me up and asking me to help them out.'

I didn't even have the energy to roll my eyes.

'How many martinis did you make me drink last night?'

'Me? It wasn't me that insisted on another round, or the next, or the next…I asked you if you were sure, and you said that you were. Absolutely sure, you said,' he reminded me virtuously, and I hated the laughter in his voice.

I only had the vaguest memory of getting home the night before. Phin. A taxi. Anne's astonished face as I reeled in the door.

'Oh, God…I'm going to be a statistic,' I moaned into the desk. 'I'll be one of those moody binge drinkers we're always hearing about who throw away their entire careers.'

'You don't think you might be exaggerating just a teeny bit?' said Phin. 'Letting your hair down once in a while isn't the end of the world.'

It certainly felt like the end of the world to me. I'd never been closer to pulling a sickie. I couldn't even *imagine* a time when I would feel better. My forehead stayed where it was, pressing into the desk. 'If you knew how awful I felt, you wouldn't say that.'

'You were great fun,' he offered, but that was no consolation to me then. 'You were the life and soul of the bar by the time I managed to bundle you into a taxi. It's one of the best nights I've had in a long time. I think I'm going to enjoy going out with you.'

'I'm not going out ever again,' I vowed.

'You'll have to. How else will everyone know how in love we are?'

Very cautiously, I turned my head on the desk and squinted up at him. 'Please tell me last night was all a bad dream.'

'Certainly not!' said Phin briskly. 'We had a deal. You drank to it—several times, if I recall. Besides, we're committed. I met Lex on my way in and asked if I could take you to some drinks party he's having on Friday.'

'What?' Horrified, I straightened too suddenly, and yelped as my head jarred.

'Our cunning plan is never going to work if you hide away,' Phin pointed out, sitting on the edge of my desk and deliberately pushing a pile of square-cut folders aside. I was in such a bad state that I didn't even straighten them, and he looked at me in concern.

'Jonathan will be there,' he added, to tempt me, but I was beyond comfort by then.

'Oh, God.' I collapsed back onto the desk. 'What did Lex say? He must have been horrified.'

'Not at all. He was surprised, sure, but he said falling for you could be the most sensible thing I'd ever done.'

'I can't believe I let you talk me into this,' I moaned.

'Now, come along—you'll feel better when you've had some sugar,' said Phin, jumping off the desk. 'I'll go and make some coffee, and you can have your doughnut early.'

Oddly enough, I *did* feel a bit better after something to eat. My head was still thumping, but at least it didn't feel as if it was about to fall off my neck any more.

Gingerly, I settled down at my computer and managed a few e-mails, although the clatter of the keyboard made me wince and I had to type very, very slowly, while Phin drip-fed me coffee and tried to rouse me by pretending to put files away in the wrong drawer.

'Don't torture me,' I grumbled. 'I thought you were supposed to be in love with me?'

'That's true. I should think of a truly romantic gesture to show what you mean to me. I could start putting my books in alphabetical order, or using a square rule to tidy my desk.'

'Why don't you try leaving *my* desk alone, for a start?' I said, swatting his hand aside as he made to pick up my calculator.

'Aha, I see you're feeling better!'

'I'm not. I'm a sick woman. I can't take any more.'

The words were barely out of my mouth before 'more' arrived—much more—in the shape of my mother.

She wafted in the door, beaming. 'Summer, darling, *there* you are!'

'Mum!'

It was Phin's turn to gape. *'Mum?'*

I couldn't blame him for looking staggered. No one ever believes she's my mother. You'd never think she was in her forties. She's got long red hair, shining eyes and a clear happy face. There's something fey, almost childlike, about her. I've never seen her in a scrap of make-up, she wears sandals and flowing ethnic skirts, and she always looks wonderful.

And, while she may be deeply into all things spiritual, she's not immune to flattery either. The smile she gave Phin was positively flirtatious. 'I hope I'm not interrupting?'

'Of course not,' said Phin, leaping forward to shake her hand. 'I'm Phin Gibson.'

'And I'm Starlight,' she told him.

They beamed at each other. I judged it was time to put a stop to their mutual love-in.

'I wasn't expecting you,' I said.

'I did tell you I was coming to London,' she reminded me.

She *had* said something, I remembered too late. 'I didn't realise it would be so soon.'

'It was an impulse.'

When had it ever *not* been an impulse? I thought wearily.

'We were gathered the other evening, channelling, when we were all seized by the same idea. It was the most extraordinary coincidence, so we knew that it had to be meant! Each of us felt our guardian angels were telling us to follow the ley lines into London…and now here we are!'

'What about the shop?' I asked, my heart sinking. A couple of years ago she had decided that she would open a New Age shop in Taunton. I'd been all for the idea of her settling to a job, so I'd helped with the practicalities of arranging the lease and sorting out a set-up loan. Mum had been full of enthusiasm for a while, but I hadn't heard much about it recently. Obviously she was into something else now.

Sure enough, she waved all talk of the shop aside. 'This is more important, Summer. We've been walking between the worlds at the power-sites along the ley line. The earth needs it desperately at the moment. Only by channelling the energy and letting the Divine Will flow through us can we help to heal it.'

'Someone told me there's a ley line running right along the Mall to Buckingham Palace,' said Phin, sounding interested. 'Is that right?'

'It is.' She beamed approvingly at him. 'And this building sits on the very same line! I'm getting good vibes here.'

I dropped my head into my hands. My hangover had come back with a vengeance. I wasn't up to dealing with my mother today. I wished Phin would stop encouraging her.

Meanwhile my mother had turned her attention back to me. 'Your aura is looking very murky, Summer. Haven't you been using the crystals I sent you? If only I had some jade with me. That's very calming for irritability.'

'I'm not irritable, Mum,' I said—irritably. 'I've just got a bit of headache.'

'I sense your energy is all out of balance.' She tutted. 'You need to realign your chakras.'

'Right, I'll do that. Look, Mum, it's lovely to see you, but I have to get on. Where are you staying? We could meet up this evening.'

Her face fell. 'Jemima is going to regress tonight. Her spiritual journeys are always *so* interesting,' she told Phin. 'Last time she was reborn as one of Cleopatra's maids. It was quite an eye-opener.'

'I can imagine,' he said. 'You wouldn't want to miss that, so why don't I take you both out to lunch?'

'Oh, but—' I began in dismay, but neither Phin nor my mother were listening.

'I know a vegan restaurant just round the corner,' he was telling her, having accurately guessed her tastes. 'They do a great line in nut cutlets.'

How Phin came to know a vegan restaurant I'll never know, as I'd had him down squarely as a steak and chips man, but sure enough, tucked away a block or two from the office, there was a little café. Before I knew it, we were tucking into grilled tofu, bean ragout and steamed brown rice, and my mother, blossoming under Phin's attention, was well into her stride with stories about my childhood. I gazed glumly into my carrot juice and wished for the oblivion of another martini.

'She was such a funny little thing,' Mum told Phin. 'Always worrying! Ken and I used to joke that her first words were "Have you paid the electricity bill?"' She laughed merrily.

'Ken was my father,' I explained to Phin. 'He died when I was nine.'

'Such a spiritual man!' My mother sighed. 'I know I should be glad he's moved on to a higher astral plane, but I still miss him sometimes. We were totally in harmony, physically and spiritually.'

'You're lucky to have had that,' said Phin gently. 'It's quite rare, I think.'

'I know, and I'm so glad dear Summer is going to have the same feeling with you.'

I looked up from the alfalfa sprouts I was pushing around my plate, startled. 'Er, Mum, I think you've got wrong end of the stick. Phin's my boss.'

I might as well have spared my breath. 'His colours are very strong,' she said, and turned to him. 'I'm getting a lot of yellow from you.'

'Is that good?' asked Phin, as if he was really interested.

'In positive aspects, absolutely. Yellow is a warm colour. It relates to the personality, the ego.'

'No wonder you've got so much of it,' I said snippily, but Phin held up a hand.

'Hold on, I get the feeling your mother really understands me.'

'Yellow is how we feel about ourselves and about others.' Did I tell you Mum is a colour therapist? 'It tells me that you're confident and wise and positive about life.'

'And you thought I was just like everyone else,' Phin said to me. 'What about Summer? Is she as wise as me?'

'Summer has a cool aura,' said Mum, well away now. 'She's got a lot of indigo and blue. That means she's fearless and dutiful and self-sacrificing, but she's also kind and practical.'

Phin nudged me. 'Bet you wish you were wise, like me!'

'You're a very good match,' Mum said, and I scowled.

'How do you work that out? Yellow and blue are quite different.'

'But when you put them together they make green,' said my mother. 'That's the colour of balance and harmony.' She smiled at us both. 'Green relates to the heart chakra, too. When it comes to giving and receiving love, it's the perfect combination.'

'Thank you for not laughing at her,' I said to Phin when my mother had drifted off to prepare for the evening's regression. I fingered the clear crystal pendulum ("Very good for energy tuning") that she had pressed on me before she left. 'I know she's a bit wacky, but…'

'But she's so shiningly sincere you can't help but like her,' said Phin. 'What's not to like about someone who loves life as much as she does?'

As we walked back to the office I tried to imagine Jonathan sitting down to grilled tofu with my mother. I'd never really talked to him about my childhood. I'd had the feeling he'd be appalled by her flaky ideas, and I was absurdly grateful to Phin for seeing her good side.

'It must have been hard for you, losing your father when you were so young.' Phin broke into my thoughts. 'Did you miss him?'

'Not that much,' I said honestly. 'We were living in a commune then, and there were lots of other people around. Besides, we weren't allowed to be sad. We had to rejoice that he had ascended to a higher plane.'

I shook my head, remembering. 'I think it must have been much harder for my mother. They do seem to have really loved each other, and I suspect she threw herself into the spiritual side of things as a way of coping. She's got a very flimsy grasp on reality, and sometimes she drives me mad, but at least she's happy.' I sighed. 'And who am I to say what she should or shouldn't believe?'

'I can't see you in a commune,' Phin commented.

'I hated it, but, looking back, it was the best place for Mum,' I said reflectively. 'I wish she'd join another. At least then someone else would worry about the day-to-day things.'

'Like paying the electricity bill?'

'Exactly. They were both hopeless with money, and just couldn't be bothered with things like bills, so the electricity was always getting cut off. They thought it was funny that I used to fret, but if I didn't sort out the practicalities no one else would.'

'Sounds like they were the opposite of my parents,' said Phin, as we waited to cross the road at the lights. 'They were both obsessed with financial security. They thought that as long as they could pay for us to go to "good" schools and we had everything we wanted they would have done their duty as parents.'

He grinned at me suddenly. 'We're an ungrateful generation, aren't we? My parents did their best, just like yours did. It's not their fault that we want different things from them. Mine drive me mad, just like your mother does you, but that doesn't mean I don't love them. The truth is that there's part of me that still craves their approval. Why else would I be at Gibson & Grieve, getting in Lex's way?'

'At least you're trying,' I said. 'My mother would be delighted if I gave up my job to channel angels or dowse for fairy paths. I don't think she even knows what "career" means.'

We were passing a burger bar just then, and as the smell of barbecued meat wafted out Phin stopped and sniffed appreciatively. 'Mmm, junk food…!' His eyes glinted as he looked down at me. 'Are you still hungry?'

'What? After all those delicious alfalfa sprouts? How can you even ask?'

We took our burgers away and sat on the steps in front of the National Gallery, looking down over Trafalgar Square. It was a bright February day, and an unseasonal warmth in the air taunted us with the promise of spring.

I was certainly feeling a lot better than I had earlier that morning. I was still a bit fuzzy round the edges but my headache had almost gone. Perhaps my mother's crystal was working after all.

'What are you doing?' Phin demanded as I unwrapped my burger and separated the bun carefully.

'I don't like the pickle,' I said, picking it out with a grimace and looking around for somewhere to dispose of it.

'Here, give it to me,' he said with a roll of his eyes, and when I passed it over he shoved it into his own burger and took a huge bite.

'See—we're like a real couple already,' he said through a mouthful.

I wished he hadn't reminded me of the crazy pretence we'd embarked upon the night before. I couldn't believe I'd actually agreed to it. I kept waiting for Phin to tell me that it was all a big joke, that he'd just been having me on.

'Did you really tell Lex that we were going out?'

'Uh-huh.' He glanced down at me. 'I told him that we were madly in love.'

I wanted to look away, but my eyes snagged on his and it was as if all the air had been suddenly sucked out of my lungs. Held by the blueness and the glinting laughter, I could only sit there and stare back at him, feeling giddy and yet centred at the same time.

It was a very strange sensation. I was acutely aware of the coldness of the stone steps, of the breeze in my face and the smell of the burger in my hands.

I did eventually manage to wrench my gaze

away, but it was an effort, and I had to concentrate on my breathing as I watched the tourists milling around the square. They held their digital cameras at arm's length, posing by the great stone lions or squinting up at Nelson on his column. A squabble erupted amongst the pigeons below us, and my eyes followed the red buses heading down Whitehall, but no matter where I looked all I saw was Phin's image, as if imprinted behind my eyelids: the mobile mouth with its lazy lop-sided smile, the line of his cheek, the angle of his jaw.

When had he become so familiar? When had I learnt exactly how his hair grew? When had I counted the creases at the edges of his eyes?

There was a yawning feeling in the pit of my stomach. Desperately I tried to conjure up Jonathan's image instead, but it was hopeless.

'What did Lex say?' I asked, struggling to sound normal. 'Did he believe you?'

'Of course he did. Why wouldn't he?'

'You've got to admit that we make an unlikely couple.'

'Your mother doesn't think so,' Phin reminded me.

'My mother believes that fairies dance around

the flowers at dawn,' I pointed out. 'The word "unlikely" doesn't occur in her vocabulary.'

'Well, Lex didn't seem at all surprised—except maybe that you would fall in love with me.' Phin crumpled the empty paper in his hand. 'He seemed to think that you were too sensible to do anything like that. He's obviously never seen you drinking pomegranate martinis!'

I flushed. If I never touched a martini again, it would be too soon.

'I would have thought he'd be more surprised that you'd be in love with *me*,' I said, finishing my own burger.

Phin shrugged. 'I'm always falling in and out of love. I suspect he's more worried that I might hurt you. He knows I'm not the settling down type. When you dump me for Jonathan, he'll probably be relieved.'

CHAPTER SIX

THE *Glitz* interview was scheduled for the next day.

Phin lived just off the King's Road, in one of those houses I have long coveted, with painted brick and colourful doors. That morning, though, I was in no mood to admire the prettiness of the street, or the window boxes filled with early daffodils that adorned the cottages on either side. I was feeling ridiculously nervous as I stood on the steps outside his door—a bright red—and I wasn't even sure why.

Except that's not quite true. I *did* know why. It was because of this crazy pretence we had agreed on. I couldn't understand how I had let myself get sucked into it. It was utter madness. *And* it would never work. I should just accept that Jonathan didn't love me and move on.

But instead I was committed to pretending to

be Phin's girlfriend. It was too late to change my mind. Phin had told Lex that we were madly in love—just imagining a conversation like that with our dour Chief Executive made my mind boggle—and now everybody knew.

Phin had rested his hand against casually against my neck as we'd waited for the lifts on our way back from Trafalgar Square. I knew he was only doing it so that Michaela at Reception would see and pass the word around—she had, and I'd only been back at my desk five minutes when Ellie was on the phone demanding to know what was going on—so there was no reason for my nape to be tingling still, no reason for me to be tense and jittery.

But I was.

Well, I had to get on with it. Drawing a deep breath, I rang the bell.

The door opened as suddenly as a slap, and there was Phin, smiling at me, in faded jeans and a T-shirt. His feet were bare, his hair rumpled, and he was in need of a shave. He looked a mess, in fact, but all at once there wasn't enough air to breathe and my mouth dried.

I badly wanted to retreat down the steps, but

pride kept me at the top. 'Hi,' I said, horrified to hear how husky my voice sounded.

'Hey,' said Phin, and before I realised what he meant to do he had kissed me on the mouth.

It was only a brief brush of the lips, the casual kind of kiss a man like Phin would bestow a hundred times at a party, but my pulse jolted as if from a massive bolt of electricity. So that's what it's like being struck by lightning. I swear every hair on my body stood up.

'What was that for?' I asked unsteadily.

'Just getting into character,' he said cheerfully. 'I hadn't realised the perks of promoting G&G's family-friendly image until now. Who would have thought it would be so much fun keeping Lex happy?'

He stood back and held the door open. 'Come on in and see where we're having our wild affair.'

We won't be able to keep our hands off each other. I remembered Phin answering my stupid question about how we would go about having an affair. *The moment we're through the front door I'll start kissing you, and you'll kiss me back. You'll fall back against the door and pull me with you...*

Now I couldn't help glancing at the door as I passed, couldn't help imagining what it would be like to feel the hard wood digging into my back, the weight of Phin's body pressing me against it, his mouth on mine, his hands hot and hungry.

I swallowed hard. I had no intention of giving Phin the satisfaction of knowing how that casual kiss had affected me, but it was difficult when I still had that weird, jerky, twitchy, shocked feeling beneath my skin.

It wasn't a very big house. Clearly it had once been a cottage, but the kitchen had been extended at the back with a beautiful glass area, and on a sunny February morning it looked bright and inviting.

'Nice house,' I managed, striving for a nonchalant tone that didn't quite come off.

'I can't take any credit for it,' said Phin. 'It was like this when I bought it. I wanted somewhere that didn't need anything doing to it. I'm not into DIY or nest-building.'

'Or tidying, by the looks of it,' I said as I wandered into the living room. Two smaller rooms that had been knocked into one, it ran from the front of the house to the back, where dust motes danced in the early spring sunshine that shone in through the window.

It could have been a lovely room, but there was stuff everywhere. A battered hat sat jauntily on the back of an armchair. The sofa was covered with newspapers. Books were crammed onto a low table with dirty mugs, empty beer cans and a water purification kit.

I clicked my tongue disapprovingly. 'How on earth do you ever find anything?'

'I've got a system,' said Phin.

'Clearly it doesn't involve putting anything away!'

He made a face. 'There never seems much point. As far as I'm concerned, this is just some-where to pack and unpack between trips.'

'What a shame.' It seemed a terrible waste to me. 'I'd love to live somewhere like this,' I said wistfully. 'This is my fantasy house, in fact.'

'The one you're saving up for?'

The chances of me ever being able to afford a house in Chelsea were so remote that I laughed. '*Fantasy*, I said! I'm saving for a studio at the end of a tube line, which will be all I can afford. And I'll be lucky if I can do that with London prices the way they are. But if I won the Lottery I'd buy a house just like this,' I said, turning slowly around and half closing my eyes as I visualised how it would be. 'I'd paint the front door blue and have window boxes at every window.'

'What's wrong with red?'

'Nothing. It's just that when I was a kid and used to dream about living in a proper house it always had a blue door, and I always swore that if I ever had a home of my own the door would be blue. I'd open it up, and inside it would be all light and stripped floorboards and no clutter…like this room could be if there wasn't all this mess!'

'It's not messy,' Phin protested. 'It's comfortable.'

'Yes, well, comfortable or not, we're going to have to clear up before Imelda and the photographer get here.'

I started to gather up the papers scattered over the sofa, but Phin grabbed them from me. 'Whoa—no, you don't!' he said firmly. 'I'll never find anything again if you start tidying. I thought we agreed the idea was to let readers see me at home?'

'No, the *idea* is that readers have a glimpse of what their lives could be like if only they shopped at Gibson & Grieve all the time,' I reminded him. 'You're a TV personality, for heaven's sake! You know how publicity works. It's about creating an image, not showing reality.'

Ignoring his grumbles, I collected up all the mugs I could find and carried them through to the kitchen. I was glad to have something to do to take my mind off the still buzzy aftermath of that kiss. I was desperately aware of Phin, and the intimacy of the whole situation, and at least I could try and disguise it with briskness.

'We'll need to offer them coffee,' I said, dumping the dirty mugs on the draining board. 'Have you got any fresh?'

'Somewhere…' Phin deposited a pile of newspapers on a chair and opened the fridge. It was like a cartoon bachelor's fridge, stacked with beers and little else, but he found a packet of ground coffee, which he handed to me, and sniffed at a carton. 'The milk seems OK,' he said. 'There should be a cafetière around somewhere, too.'

It was in the sink, still with coffee grounds at the bottom. I dreaded to think how long it had been there. Wrinkling my nose, I got rid of the grounds in the bin and washed up the cafetière with the mugs.

'What sort of state is the rest of the house in?' I asked when I had finished.

'I haven't quite finished unpacking from Peru,' Phin said as he opened the door to his bedroom.

'Quite' seemed an understatement to me. There were clothes strewn everywhere, along with various other strange items that were presumably essential when you were hacking your way through the rainforest: a mosquito net, a machete, industrial strength insect repellent. You could barely see that it was an airy room, sparsely but stylishly furnished, and dominated by an invitingly wide bed which I carefully averted my eyes from.

Phin had no such qualms. 'That's where we make mad, passionate love,' he said. 'Most of the time,' he added, seeing me purse my lips and unable to resist teasing. 'Of course there's always the shower and the sofa—and remember that time up on the kitchen table…?'

'It sounds very unhygienic,' I said crisply. 'I'd never carry on like that.'

'You would if you really wanted me.'

'Luckily for you,' I said, 'I'm only interested in your mind.'

'Don't tell *Glitz* that,' said Phin, his eyes dancing. 'You'll ruin my reputation.'

'They're not going to be interested in our sex life, anyway.'

'Summer, what world are you living in? That's *exactly* what they'll be interested in! They're journalists on a celebrity rag. I can tell you now this Imelda won't give two hoots about our minds!'

I lifted my chin stubbornly. 'The interview is supposed to be about you as a potential family man, not as some sex symbol.'

'You know, sex is an important part of marriage,' he said virtuously. 'We don't want them thinking we're not completely compatible in every way.'

'Yes, well, let's concentrate on our compatibility in the living room rather than the bedroom,' I said, closing the bedroom door. 'We'll just have to hope that they don't want to come upstairs.'

Anxious to get away from the bedroom, with all its associations, I hurried back downstairs.

'We're going to have to do something about this room,' I decided, surveying the living room critically. 'It's not just the mess. It looks too much like a single guy's room at the moment.'

I made Phin clear away all the clutter—I think he just dumped it all in the spare room—while I ran around with a vacuum cleaner. It didn't look too bad by the time I'd finished, although even I thought it was a bit bare.

'It could do with some flowers, or a cushion or two,' I said. 'Do you think I've got time to nip out before they get here?'

'Cushions?' echoed Phin, horrified. 'Over my dead body!'

'Oh, don't be such a baby. A couple of cushions wouldn't kill you.'

'Cushions are the beginning of the end,' he said mulishly. 'Next thing I know I'll be buying scented candles and ironing my sheets!'

'Sheets feel much nicer when they're ironed,' I pointed out, but he only looked at me in disbelief.

'I might as well be married. I've seen it happen

to friends,' he told me. 'They meet a fabulous girl, they're having a great time, and then one day you go round and there's a cushion sitting on the sofa. You know it's the beginning of the end. You can count the days before that wedding invitation is dropping onto your mat!'

I rolled my eyes. I was feeling much better by that stage. I always find cleaning very comforting.

'Oh, very well, it's not as if we're supposed to be married,' I conceded. 'You'll just have to look as if you're keen enough on me to be considering a cushion some time soon.'

'I think I can manage looking keen,' said Phin, and something in his voice made me glance at him sharply. Amusement and something else glimmered in the depths of those blue eyes. Something that made my breath hitch and my heart thud uneasily in my throat. Something that sent me skittering right back to square one.

I moistened my lips, and cast around wildly for something to say. 'Shouldn't you go and change?' To my horror, my voice sounded high and tight.

'What for?' said Phin easily. 'They want to see me at home, don't they?'

'Well, yes, but you might want to look as if you've made a bit of an effort. You haven't even got any shoes on. You look as if you've just rolled out of bed,' I said, and then winced inwardly, wishing I hadn't mentioned bed.

'That's what we want them to think,' said Phin. 'And, now you come to mention it, I think you're the one who needs to do something about your appearance.'

'What do you mean?' Diverted, I peered anxiously into the mirror above the mantelpiece. Anne and I had spent hours the evening before, going through the clothes heaped on my bed and trying to pick just the right look. It had to be sexy enough for me to be in with a remote chance of being Phin's girlfriend, but at the same time I wanted it to fit with Gibson & Grieve's new family-friendly image.

'And you mustn't wear black or white next to your face,' Anne had said bossily. 'It's very draining in photographs. You want to look casual, but sophisticated, elegant, but colourful, sexy, but sensible.'

In the end we had decided on a pair of black wool trousers with a silky shirt I had worn to various Christmas parties the previous December. It was a lovely cherry-red, and I had painted my nails with Anne's favourite colour, Berry Bright, to match. I had even clipped my hair up loosely, the way I wore it at the weekend. I thought I looked OK.

'What's wrong with how I look?' I asked.

'You look much too neat and tidy,' said Phin, putting his hands on either side of my waist. 'Come here.'

'What are you doing?' I asked nervously as he drew me towards him.

'I'm going to make you look as you've just rolled out of bed, too. As if we rolled out of bed together.'

Lifting one hand, he pulled the clip from my hair so that it slithered forward. 'You shouldn't hide it away,' he said, twining his fingers through it. 'It's beautiful stuff. I thought it was just brown at first, but every time I look at it I see a different colour. Sometimes it looks gold, sometimes chestnut, sometimes honey. I swear I've even seen red in there...it makes me think of an autumn wood.'

I was speechless—and not just because of his closeness, which was making me feel hazy. No one had ever said anything like that to me before. I didn't want to look into his eyes to see if he was joking or not. I was afraid that if I did I would lose what little grip I still had on my senses.

'Very poetic,' I managed.

'But it'll look even more beautiful tousled up,' said Phin—and, ignoring my protests, he mussed up my hair before turning his attention to my shirt. 'And, yes…I think we'll have to do something about this, too. There are just too many buttons done up here, and they're all done up the right way! That won't do at all.'

Very slowly, very deliberately, he undid the first two buttons and looked down at me, his eyes dark and blue.

'No, you still look horribly cool,' he said, which must have been a lie because my heart was thundering in my chest and I was burning where those blunt, surprisingly deft fingers had grazed my skin. I opened my mouth, but the words jammed in my throat, piling into an inarticulate sound that fell somewhere between a squeak and a gasp. He was barely touching me, but every cell in my body was screaming with awareness and I couldn't have moved if I had tried.

'I may have to work a bit harder on this one…'
he went on and, bending his head, he blew gently
just below my ear. The feel of it shuddered
straight down my spine and clutched convul-
sively at its base. In spite of myself, I shivered.

'Mmm, yes, this may just work,' said Phin,
pleased, and then he was trailing kisses down my
neck, warm and soft and tantalising.

I really, *really* didn't want to respond, but I
couldn't help myself. It was awful. It was as if
some other woman had taken over my body,
tipping her head back and sucking in her breath
with another shudder of excitement.

My heart was thudding in my throat, and I
could hear the blood rushing giddily in my ears.

'You see where I'm going with this,'
murmured Phin, who was managing to undo
another couple of buttons at the same time. 'I
mean, we did discuss how important it was to
make it look as if we found each other irresist-
ible, didn't we?'

'I think that's probably enough buttons,
though,' I croaked as he started on the other side
of my neck. His hair was tickling my jaw and I
could smell his shampoo. The wonderfully

clean, male scent of his skin combined with the wicked onslaught of his lips was making my head spin, and I felt giddy and boneless.

Perhaps that was why I didn't resist as Phin steered me over to the great leather sofa. There was no way my legs were going to hold me up much longer, and as we sank down onto the cushions I felt as if I were sinking into a swirl of abandon.

'OK, no more buttons,' he whispered, and I could feel his lips curving against my throat. 'But…I…don't…think…you…look…*quite*…convincing…enough…yet.'

Between each word he pressed a kiss along my jaw until he reached my mouth at last, and then his lips were on mine, and he was kissing me with an expertise that literally took my breath away. Since I'm being frank, I'll admit that it was a revelation. I'd never been kissed so surely, so thoroughly, so completely and utterly deliciously. So irresistibly.

I certainly couldn't resist it. I wound my arms around him, pulling him closer, and kissed him back.

It wasn't that I didn't know who he was or

what I was doing, but I thought… Well, I don't know what I thought, OK? The truth is, I wasn't thinking at all. I was just *feeling*, the slither of the satiny shirt against my skin, the hardness and heat of his hands on me as he pushed the slippery material aside.

Just tasting…his mouth, his skin.

Just hearing the wild rush of my pulse, the uneven way he said my name, my own ragged breathing.

Just *touching*—fumbling at his T-shirt, tugging it up so that I could run my hands feverishly over his smoothly muscled back, marvelling at the way it flexed beneath my fingers. I let them drift up the warmth of his flanks and felt him shiver in response.

What can I say? I was lost, astonished at my own abandon, and yet helpless to pull myself back.

Or perhaps I'm not being *entirely* honest. I was aware at one level of my sensible self frantically waving her arms and ordering me back to safety, but Phin's body felt so good, so lean and hard as it pressed me into the sofa, and his mouth was so wickedly enticing, that I ignored her and let my fingers drift to the fastening of his jeans instead.

Afterwards, I could hardly believe it, but the truth is that there was a moment when I *did* know that I'd regret it later, and I still chose the lure of Phin's hands taking me to places I'd barely suspected before. I succumbed to the excitement rocketing through me, and if Imelda and the photographer hadn't arrived just then who knows where we would have ended up?

Except I do know, of course.

What I don't know is whether that would have been a good thing or a bad thing. I'm pretty sure I would have enjoyed it, though.

As it was, the piercing ring of the doorbell tore through the hazy pleasure and brought me right back to earth with a sickening crash.

I jerked bolt upright. 'Oh, my God, it's them!'

Frantically I tried to button up my shirt and shove it back into my trousers at the same time as pushing my hair behind my ears. 'What were we *doing*?'

Phin was infuriatingly unperturbed. He was barely breathing unsteadily. 'Well, I don't know about you, but *I've* been doing my bit for our pretence—and with all due modesty, I think I've excelled,' he said, and grinned as his eyes rested on my face. I dreaded to think what I looked like. 'Now you really *do* look the part.'

The bell rang again, more stridently this time. 'Ready?' asked Phin, and without waiting for me to answer strolled to open the door.

I could hear him exchanging chit-chat with Imelda and the photographer in the narrow hallway as I desperately tried to compose myself. I was horrified when I looked in the mirror to see that my hair was all over the place, my eyes huge and my lips swollen. I hardly recognised myself. I looked wild. I looked wanton.

I looked *sexy*.

I looked the part, just like Phin had said.

The next moment Phin was ushering Imelda into the room. She stopped when she saw me. 'Hello,' she said, obviously surprised.

'Hello,' I said weakly, and then remembered— far too late, I know—that I was the one who had set up this interview. I cleared my throat and stepped forward to shake her hand. 'We've spoken on the phone,' I said. 'I'm Summer Curtis—Phin's PA.'

'Ah.' Imelda looked amused, and when I followed her gaze I saw that she was looking at my shirt, which I had managed to button up all wrong in my haste.

Flushing, I made to fix the top button, and then realised that I was just going to get into an awful muddle unless I undid them all and started again. As Phin had no doubt intended.

'Not just my PA,' said Phin, coming to put his arm round my waist and pulling me into his side.

'So I see,' said Imelda dryly.

Her elegant brows lifted in surprise. I didn't blame her. She must have known as well as I did that I wasn't exactly Phin's usual type, and I lost confidence abruptly. We'd never be able to carry this off. Not in front of someone as sharp as Imelda.

'Shall I make coffee?' I asked quickly, desperate to get out of the room. My heart was still crashing clumsily around in my chest, and I was having a lot of trouble breathing. I felt trembly and jittery, and I kept going hot and cold as if I had a fever.

Perhaps I *did* have a fever? I latched onto the thought as I filled the kettle with shaking hands. That would explain the giddiness, the way I had melted into Phin with barely a moment's hesitation. My cheeks burned at the memory.

Not just my cheeks, to be honest.

When I came back in with a tray, having taken the opportunity to refasten my shirt and tuck myself in properly, Phin was leaning back on the sofa, looking completely relaxed. He pulled me down onto the sofa beside him. 'Thanks, babe,' he said, and rested a hand possessively on my thigh.

Babe? Ugh. I was torn between disgust and an agonising awareness of his hand touching my leg. It felt as if it were burning a hole through my trousers, and I was sure that when I took them off I would find an imprint of his palm scorched onto my skin.

'So, Phin,' said Imelda, when we had got the whole business of passing around the milk and sugar out of the way. 'It sounds as if you're making a lot of changes in your life right now. Does your new role at Gibson & Grieve mean you're ready to stop travelling?'

'I won't stop completely,' he said. 'I've still got various programme commitments, and besides, I'm endlessly curious about the world. There are still so many wonderful places to see, and so many exciting things to do. I'm never going to turn my back on all that completely. Having said that, my father's stroke did make me reassess my priorities. Gibson & Grieve is part of my life, and it feels good to be involved in the day to day running of it. It's time for me to do my part, instead of leaving it all to my brother.

'And then, of course, there's Summer.' He lifted my hand and pressed a kiss it. His lips were warm and sure, and a shiver travelled down my spine. I did my best to disguise it by shifting on the sofa, but I saw Imelda look at me. 'She's changed everything for me.'

'You're thinking of settling down?' She made a moue of exaggerated disappointment. 'That's another of the most eligible bachelors off the available list!'

'I'm afraid so,' said Phin, entwining his fingers with mine. 'I was always afraid of the idea of settling down, but since I've met Summer it doesn't seem so much like giving up my freedom as finding what I've been looking for all these years.'

You've got to admit he was good. No one could have guessed he'd been ranting about cushions and commitment only a few minutes earlier.

Imelda was lapping it all up, while I sat with

a stupid smile on my face, not knowing what to do with my expression. Should I look besotted? Shy? Smug?

'You're a lucky woman.' Imelda turned to me. 'What's it like knowing that half the women in the country would like to be in your place?'

I cleared my throat. 'To be honest, it hasn't sunk in yet. It's still very new.'

'But it feels absolutely right, doesn't it?' Phin put in.

He was doing so much better than me that I felt I should make an effort. 'Yes,' I said slowly, 'funnily enough, it does.'

And then, bizarrely, it didn't seem so difficult. I smiled at him, and he smiled back, and for a long moment we just looked at each other and there was nothing but the blueness of his eyes and the thud of my heart and the air shortening around us.

It took a pointed cough from Imelda to jerk me back to reality. With an effort, I dragged my eyes from Phin's and tried to remember what I was supposed to be talking about. Phin, that was it. Phin and me and our supposed passion for each other.

'We're so different in lots of ways,' I told Imelda, and the words seemed to come unbidden. 'Phin isn't at all the kind of guy I thought I would fall in love with, but it turns out that he's exactly right for me.'

'So it wasn't love at first sight for you?'

'No, he was just…my boss.'

'And what made the difference for you?'

Images rushed through my head like the flickering pages of a book. Phin smiling. Phin wiping cream from my cheek. Phin pulling the clip from my hair. Phin's mouth and Phin's hands and the hard excitement of Phin's body.

'I…I don't know,' I said hesitantly. 'I just looked at him one day and knew that I was in love with him.'

I thought it was pretty feeble, but Imelda was nodding as if she understood and looking positively dewy-eyed.

I was all set to relax then, but that was only the beginning. I still had to endure an excruciating photo session, posing cuddled up to Phin or looking at him adoringly, and my nerves were well and truly frayed by the time it was over. I tried to get out of the photographs, pleading that the article was about Phin, not me, but Imelda was adamant.

'All our readers will want to see the lucky woman who has convinced Phin Gibson to settle down,' she insisted.

I can tell you, I didn't feel very lucky by the time we'd finished. I was exhausted by the effort of pretending to be in love with Phin, while simultaneously trying to convince him that all the touching and kissing was having no effect on me at all.

But at last it was over. We waved them off from the steps, and then Phin closed the door and grinned at me. 'Very good,' he said admiringly. 'You practically had me convinced!'

'You didn't do badly yourself,' I said. 'You weren't lying when you said you were a good actor.'

No harm in reminding him that I knew he *had* been acting.

'If you can fool a hard-boiled journalist like Imelda, you should be able to fool Jonathan,' Phin said.

Why hadn't I remembered Jonathan before? I wondered uneasily. Jonathan was the reason I was doing this. I should have been thinking about him all morning, not about the sick, churning excitement I felt when Phin kissed me.

'Let's hope so,' I said, as coolly as I could. I looked at my watch. 'We'd better get back to the office.'

'What's the rush? Let's have lunch first,' said Phin. 'We should celebrate.'

'Celebrate what?'

'A successful interview, for one thing. Promoting Gibson & Grieve's family image. And let's not forget our engagement.'

'We're not engaged,' I said repressively.

'As good as,' he said, shrugging on his jacket and slipping a wallet into the inside pocket. He held the door open for me. 'You're now officially the woman who's convinced me to settle down.'

'You may be settling down, but I'm certainly not spending my life with anyone who calls me babe!'

Phin grinned at me as he pulled the door closed behind him. 'It's a mark of affection.'

'It's patronising.'

'Well, what would you like me to call you?'

'What's wrong with my name?'

'Every self-respecting couple has special names for each other,' he pointed out.

We walked towards the King's Road. 'Well, if you have to, you can call me darling,' I allowed after a moment, but Phin shook his head, his eyes dancing.

'No, no—darling is much too restrained, too *ordinary*, for you. You're much sexier than you realise, and we need to make sure Jonathan realises, too. Shall I call you bunnikins?'

'Shall I punch you on the nose?' I retorted sweetly.

He laughed. 'Pumpkin? Muffin? Cupcake?'

'Cupcake?'

'You'd be surprised,' said Phin. 'But you're right. I don't see you as a cupcake. What about cookie?'

'Oh, please!'

'Or—I know! This is perfect for you, and in keeping with the baking theme…cream puff?'

'Don't you dare!'

'Cream puff it is,' said Phin, as if I hadn't spoken. 'All crispy on the outside, but soft and delicious in the middle. It couldn't be better for you,' he said. 'That's settled. So, what are you going to call me?'

I looked at him. 'You really—*really*—don't want to know,' I said.

CHAPTER SEVEN

PHIN only smiled and took my hand. 'Come along, my little cream puff. Let's go and find some lunch. If you don't want to celebrate our non-engagement, let's just celebrate the fact that it's a beautiful day. What more reason do we need, anyway?'

I tried to imagine Jonathan suggesting that we celebrated the fact that the sun was shining, but I couldn't do it. It wasn't that he was a killjoy. Jonathan would celebrate a promotion, a rise in profits, a successful advertising campaign, perhaps. But a lovely day? I didn't think so.

And if he did celebrate he would want to plan it. Jonathan would book the very best restaurant, or order the most expensive champagne. He wouldn't just wander along the King's Road the way Phin did, and find the first place with a table in a sunny window.

But that was why I loved Jonathan, I reminded myself hastily. I loved him precisely because he *wasn't* spontaneous, because he was the kind of man who would think things through and plan them sensibly, instead of dropping everything when the sun came out, and because he didn't act on a whim the way my mother and Phin did.

On the other hand, I have to admit that I enjoyed that lunch—although that may have been largely due to the large glass of wine that came with it. I asked for water, but the wine came, and then it seemed too much of a fuss to send it back, so I ended up drinking it. I'm not used to drinking in the middle of the day, and I could feel myself flushing, and laughing a lot more than I usually do.

Perhaps it was relief at having got through the interview. Perhaps it was the sunshine.

Or perhaps it was Phin sitting opposite me, making me believe that there was nowhere else he would rather be and no one else he would rather be with. Having spent months having to be grateful for any time Jonathan could spare me, it was a novel sensation for me to be the focus of attention for a change.

It was so little, really—to feel that Phin saw *me* when he looked at me, that he was listening, really listening, to what I was saying—but I'd have been less than human if I hadn't responded, and I could feel myself unfurling in the simple pleasure of having lunch with an attractive man on a sunny day.

It was very unlike me. I'm normally very puritanical about long lunches in office time. I wasn't myself that day.

I felt really quite odd, in fact. Fizzy, is the best way to describe it, as if that kiss had left all my senses on high alert. I was desperately aware of Phin opposite me, scanning the menu. I could see every one of the laughter lines around his eyes, the crease in his cheek, and that dent at the corner of his crooked mouth which always seemed on the point of breaking into a smile.

I was supposed to be looking at the menu, too, but I couldn't concentrate. My eyes kept flickering over to him, skittering from the prickle of stubble on his jaw to his hands, to his throat and then back to that mobile mouth. And my own mouth dried at the memory of how excitingly sure his lips had been.

My whole body still seemed to be humming with the feel of his hands, of his mouth, but at the same time it seemed hard to believe that we could have kissed like that and yet be sitting here quite normally, as if nothing had happened at all. I shifted uncomfortably as I remembered how eagerly I had kissed Phin back. What must he think of me?

On the other hand, it hadn't been a *real* kiss, had it? It hadn't meant anything. Phin had made it clear enough that he had only been kissing me for effect, and I wondered if I ought to make it clear that I had been doing the same. And, yes, I know, that wasn't exactly how it was, but a girl has her pride.

Or perhaps I should pretend to ignore the whole issue?

I was still dithering when Phin looked up from the menu. 'Have you decided? I'm going to have a starter, too. I don't know about you, but all that kissing has given me an appetite!'

Now that he had raised the subject, I thought I might as well take the opportunity to make my position quite clear.

'Speaking of kissing,' I said, and was secretly

impressed at how cool I sounded, 'perhaps we ought to discuss what happened earlier. I understand *why* you kissed me—' I went on.

Phin's brows lifted and his smile gleamed. 'Do you, now?'

'Of course. It created a convincing effect for Imelda, and I can see that it worked, but I hope there won't be any need to repeat it,' I said, at my most priggish.

Much effect it had on Phin. 'Now, there we differ, cream puff, because I hope there *will*. I enjoyed that kiss very much. Didn't you?'

My eyes darted around the table and I longed for the nerve to lie.

'I just don't want to lose sight of what we're trying to do here,' I said evasively. 'And don't call me cream puff.'

'That wasn't quite an answer to my question, though, was it?' said Phin with a provocative smile.

I might have known he wouldn't let me get away with it.

We locked eyes for a mute moment, until he gave in with a grin and a shake of his head.

'Look, don't worry. I haven't forgotten that for you this is about getting Jonathan back.'

'And it's promoting Gibson & Grieve,' I added quickly, not wanting it to be all about me. 'Not to mention keeping Jewel at arm's length!'

'All very fine causes,' Phin agreed with a virtuous expression. 'But since we're going through this pretence, it seems to me we might as well enjoy it. We're not going to look like a very convincing couple if we never touch each other, are we? Touching is what couples do.'

Jonathan and I had never touched in public. But then we hadn't been a real couple, had we?

'OK,' I said, 'but only when necessary.'

'Only when necessary,' he confirmed, and held up crossed fingers. 'Scout's honour. Now, let's get serious and talk about lunch…'

I felt that I had made my point, and after that I was able to relax a little. I suppose that glass of wine helped, too. I don't remember what we talked about—just nonsense, I think—but I was still in an uncharacteristically light-hearted mood when we made it back to the office.

We waited for a lift in the glossy atrium, with the sun angling through the building to lie across the floor in a broad stripe. Phin was telling me about a disastrous trip he'd been on for one of the

Into the Wild programmes, where everything that could possibly go wrong had done, and I was laughing when the lift pinged at last and the doors slid open to reveal Lex and Jonathan.

There was a moment of startled silence, then they stepped out. I had a sudden image of myself through Lex's eyes, flushed and laughing and dishevelled. Somewhere along the line I had mislaid my clip, and my hair was still tumbling to my shoulders. In my silky red shirt I must have looked almost unrecognisable from my usual crisp self.

My smile faded as I encountered first Lex's stern gaze, then Jonathan's astounded look.

'Hello,' said Phin cheerfully. 'Don't tell me you two are sloping off early?'

'We've got a meeting in the City.' Pointedly Lex looked at his watch and, like Pavlov's dog, I looked at mine, too. My eyes nearly started out of my head when I saw that it was almost three o'clock. How had it got that late?

'I see you're not letting your new position here change your work ethic,' he added, with one of his trademark sardonic looks.

Phin was unperturbed. 'Less of the sarcasm,

please,' he said. He was the only person I knew who wasn't the slightest bit intimidated by Lex. I suppose it helped that Lex was his brother. 'I'll have you know we've been busy promoting Gibson & Grieve all morning.'

'It's some time since morning,' said Lex, less than impressed.

'We've been recovering from the stress of persuading the media of my family friendly credentials. Summer did an absolutely brilliant job.'

I wished he hadn't mentioned me. Lex's cold grey gaze shifted back to me, and it took all I had not to squirm. I was unnervingly aware of Jonathan's astounded gaze fixed on me, too. I managed a weak smile.

'Remarkable,' was all Lex said.

'Isn't she?' said Phin fondly, putting an arm around me and pulling me against him. I could feel the heat and weight of his hand at my waist, making the slippery material of my shirt shift over my skin. 'That's just what I've been telling her.'

'We're so late,' I wailed as soon as we got in the lift. I could feel myself winding rapidly back up to my usual self. I was *never* late. Well, there had been yesterday, after the pomegranate

martinis, but that had been exceptional circumstances. I couldn't believe that I had actually sat
there in the sun and let time tick by without even
thinking about getting back to the office.

'We're not late,' said Phin. 'We haven't got
any appointments this afternoon.'

'I should have been back earlier,' I fretted, remembering Jonathan and Lex's raised brows. 'I
wish they hadn't seen me like this,' I said as I
tugged my shirt into place. 'I look so unprofessional.'

'Nonsense. You look fantastic,' said Phin. 'We
couldn't have planned it better if we had tried.
Did you *see* Jonathan's expression?'

I nodded. 'He was horrified,' I said gloomily.

'He wasn't horrified. He was absolutely
amazed.' Phin spoke with complete authority.
'He looked at you and saw exactly what he could
have had if he'd ever taken the trouble to kiss you
senseless on a sofa and then take you out to lunch.
He didn't like me touching you either,' he added.

'How on earth do you know that?'

'It's a guy thing.' Phin smiled smugly. 'Trust
me, Summer, our little plan is working already.'

I know I should have been delighted, but

actually I spent the rest of the afternoon feeling scratchy and unsettled. It was impossible to concentrate. It wasn't fair, the way Phin could be so casual about it all. How could he kiss me like that and then turn round and sound pleased at the idea of handing me on to someone else?

Easily, of course. It was a guy thing, just like he had said. Phin was perfectly happy to enjoy a kiss, or a long lunch, as long as there was no suggestion of any long-term commitment.

I'm not the settling down type, he had said. Well, no surprises there. And no reason for his cheerful admission to leave me feeling not *depressed*, exactly, but just a bit…flat.

I told myself not to be so silly.

So there we were, in this ridiculous situation, working together as boss and PA during the day, and at night pretending to be madly in love.

Whenever I stopped to think about what we were doing I wondered what on earth had possessed me to agree to such a thing, so it was easier to carry on as if it were perfectly normal to spend your days talking to your boss about brand marketing or strategic development or the logistics of taking twenty people to Africa to help build a medical centre, and your nights holding his hand and leaning into his warm, solid body as if you knew it as well as your own.

It was a strange time, but the funny thing was it really did seem quite normal after a while. I couldn't understand why everybody else didn't see through the pretence right away, but they all seemed to accept it without question. It was bizarre.

I was so unlike Phin's normal girlfriends, most of whom he still seemed to get on excellently with. To a woman, they were lushly glamorous and prone to extravagant kisses, with much 'mwah-mwah' and many 'darlings' scattered around. Next to them, I felt prim and boring. I tried to loosen up, but every time Phin put his arm around me or took my hand my senses would snarl into a knot and I would prickle all over with awareness. It wasn't exactly relaxing.

The first night we appeared as a couple we went to a party, to launch some perfume, I think. Something unlikely, anyway. I can remember wondering why on earth Phin had been invited, but he seemed to be on hobnobbing terms with all sorts of celebrities. That was also the first time I realised quite how many ex-girlfriends he had, and I was glad I hadn't done anything silly like let myself wonder if that kiss might have meant something to Phin, too.

Still, I was nervous. It was all so strange to me, and I was feeling very self-conscious in a short dress with spaghetti straps which I had borrowed from Anne. It showed rather more flesh than I was used to, and when Phin let his hand slide down my spine I shivered.

He clicked his tongue. 'You're too tense,' he murmured in my ear. 'You're supposed to like me touching you.'

'Anyone would be tense, meeting all your ex-girlfriends like this,' I said out of the corner of my mouth, while keeping my smile fixed in place. 'They're all wondering what on earth you're doing with me.'

'Their boyfriends aren't.' His smile glimmered as he ran a knuckle along the neckline of my dress. 'You look delectable, in a behind-closed-doors kind of way.'

I hated the way every cell in my body seemed

to leap at his touch. It made it very hard to remember that I was in control.

'What kind of way is that?' I asked, squirming at the breathlessness in my voice.

'You know—all cool on the surface, but making every man feel that if only he were lucky enough to get you on your own you'd be every hot-blooded male's fantasy.'

'Oh, please,' I said edgily, moving away from him. 'And stop stroking me!'

'Nope,' said Phin as he pulled me easily back against him. 'You're my girlfriend, and I can't keep my hands off you!'

'You've clearly got the same problem with your ex-girlfriends too,' I said waspishly. 'I notice you're still very touchy-feely with them.'

'Could it be that you're jealous, cream puff?'

'I'm hardly likely to be jealous, am I? I'm just keeping in character, like you. I'm sure if I really was your new girlfriend I wouldn't want to see quite how chummy you still are with them.'

'I'm just saying hello to old friends.'

I sniffed. 'I can manage to say hello to friends without sticking my tongue down their throats!'

'You do exaggerate, Summer—' Phin began,

amused, and then broke off. 'Uh-oh. Do you see who I see?'

I followed his gaze to where Jewel Stevens was wrapped around a young guy who looked vaguely familiar to me. I wondered if I'd seen him on television. He was very pretty, but had a vacuous look about him.

'That's Ricky Roland,' said Phin in my ear. 'He's a rising star, they say, and just as well if he's going to get involved with Jewel! He'll be able to afford a new dinner service. I wonder how many plates he's got left?'

'She's coming over,' I hissed as Jewel somehow spotted Phin and made a beeline for him, abandoning poor Ricky with barely a word. Phin promptly put his arm around my waist and pulled me closer, so that I was half in front of him like a shield.

'Phin, darling, where have you *been*?' she cried as she came up—and, completely ignoring my existence, she gave him a smacking kiss on the lips.

'Peru,' he said, keeping a firm hold of me.

'What on earth for?' said Jewel, but didn't bother to wait for his reply. She glanced languidly around at the party. 'This is all very tedious, isn't it? We're all going on to a club after this if you want to come.'

'Not tonight, thanks, Jewel,' said Phin, his smile steady but inflexible. 'I'm taking Summer home. You remember Summer, don't you?'

Jewel's eyes flicked over me as if I was something unpleasant Phin had brought in on the bottom of his shoe. 'No.'

Charming, I thought. 'I'm Phin's PA,' I reminded her.

'And so much more than that, too,' said Phin.

At that, Jewel's gaze sharpened, and she looked from Phin to me, and then back to Phin again. 'You and…Sunshine, or whatever her name is?' she said incredulously.

'Yes,' said Phin blandly. 'Me and Summer.'

Disconcertingly, Jewel began to laugh. 'You and your little secretary…isn't that a bit of a cliché, darling?'

Phin's arm tightened around me, but his voice was admirably even. 'That's the thing about clichés,' he said. 'They're so often true.'

'Well, if you say so.' Jewel was evidently unconvinced. Her brown eyes rested speculatively on me once more, and I could practically hear her thinking that I was too boring to hold Phin's attention for more than five minutes. 'How very odd,' she said.

And then she leant forward to Phin and did her ear licking trick again. *Bleuch*. 'When you're bored and want some excitement again, give me a call,' she said huskily, only to shriek and leap back as I moved, managing to stand on her foot and spill my glass of champagne all down her fabulous dress at the same time.

It was quite a clever move, even if I say so myself. Subtle, but effective.

'Oh, I'm *so* sorry,' I said insincerely as she glared at me. I could feel Phin's body shaking with suppressed laughter. 'How clumsy of me.'

I could see Jewel debating whether to make a scene, but in the end she just sent me a poisonous look and kissed Phin once more. On the mouth, this time, which was a fairly effective retort of her own.

'You know where to find me when you change your mind, darling,' she said to him.

My lips thinned as she prowled off to reclaim Ricky Roland, who was making the big mistake of talking to a pretty girl about his own age. I didn't fancy his chances of keeping the rest of his plates intact.

'When!' I huffed. 'She's got a nerve, hasn't she? Not even *if* you lose interest in me!'

'Yes, but the round definitely went to you, with the champagne spilling trick,' said Phin, letting me go at last. 'That was an excellent impression of a jealous girlfriend, Summer. I didn't think you had it in you!'

'I don't think it convinced Jewel,' I said. 'She clearly didn't believe for a moment that you'd be interested in anyone as boring as me!'

'No? Well, her style is much more obvious than yours.'

'You can say that again!'

He studied me for a moment. 'Personally, I think that restrained look is good for you. It's classy. On the other hand, it *would* look more natural if you could be a little more relaxed.'

'What do you mean?'

'We may have to do something about making you look a *little* less like a librarian who's strayed into an orgy,' said Phin. 'It works for me—don't get me wrong!—but other people might wonder eventually why you're so tense with me.'

'Maybe they'll think I'm shy,' I said, on the defensive. I knew I looked uptight—I *felt* uptight—but then so would you if you had to snuggle up to Phin while Jewel stuck her tongue down his ear, and I wasn't used to parties where you fell over a celebrity every time you turned round.

'You can get away with being shy tonight, but the next time we go out you'll need to loosen up a bit.'

'How do you suggest I do that?' I snapped, annoyed because I knew he was right.

'I'm not sure yet,' said Phin. 'I'll give it some thought.'

But, apart from Jewel, everyone seemed to accept our supposed relationship with an extraordinary lack of surprise. Monique, Lex's PA, whom I'd always admired for her perspicacity, even told me that she thought Phin and I were a perfect match!

'You're just right for each other,' she said when we met in the corridor one day, on my way back from making coffee. 'He's so lovely, isn't he?' she went on, while I was still boggling at the idea that anyone could think Phin and I were right for each other when it must be blindingly obvious that we were completely different.

'Lex is always baffled by him, but Phin is a huge asset to Gibson & Grieve if only he'd recognise it. He's one of those people that just has to walk into a room and everyone relaxes, because you know he'll be able to defuse any situation and charm everyone so they'll all go away feeling good about themselves, whatever's been decided.'

I did some more boggling then. Relaxed was the last thing I felt with Phin. He was too unpredictable. One minute he'd be sitting lazily with his feet up on the desk, the next he'd be fizzing with energy. I never knew when he was going to appear or what he was going to do.

Whenever Phin was around I felt edgy, jittery. My pulse was prone to kicking up a beat at the most inexplicable moments. All he had to do was stretch his arms above his head and yawn, or look at me with that smile twitching at his mouth, and my heart would start to thump and an alarming shivery feeling would uncoil in my belly and tremble outwards, until my whole skin prickled with awareness. It was very disturbing.

Relaxed? Ha!

'How are *you* anyway, Monique?' I asked, sick of being told how wonderful Phin was.

'Fantastic,' she said, beaming. 'In fact…' She checked to make sure no one else was around. 'I'm not telling many people yet, as it's early days, but I'm pregnant!'

I was delighted for her. I knew that Monique and her husband had been hoping for a baby for a while now. 'Monique, that's wonderful news! Dave must be thrilled.'

'He is. Lex is less so, of course,' she said, with a wry roll of her eyes.

Monique adored her boss, but she had no illusions about him. With Lex it was business all the way, and babies just didn't enter the equation.

'He was grumbling just this morning that if I'd told him earlier he would never have let you go and work for Phin—and what a shame that would have been!' She hesitated. 'I don't suppose you'd want to go back to Lex's office now, but he'll be looking for someone he trusts to cover my maternity leave, so if you're interested there might be an opening in a few months.'

'*Really?*'

'The baby's due in September, so I'll work up until August,' she said. 'Talk it over with Phin and see what he thinks. If you're spending all your time together, it might not be a bad thing to work in different offices…but you'd obviously want to vet any new PA!' Monique could obviously see the thoughts whirling in my brain. 'Maybe I shouldn't have said anything? I was just being selfish. It would make it so much easier for me if I could reassure Lex that you'd look after him while I'm away, that's all.'

'I'll definitely think about it,' I promised.

Thoughtfully, I carried the coffee back to my office. To be Lex's PA—the most senior in the company…! Only temporarily, of course, until Monique came back. But what a thing to have on my CV. It would be an extraordinary opportunity, and one I could only ever have dreamed of up to now.

It was hard to believe that only a month ago I had felt utterly hopeless. Now I not only had the prospect of a fantastic promotion, but there was even a real chance of getting back together with Jonathan. Or so Phin seemed to think—and, much as I hated to admit that he was right, I had to admit that Jonathan had been much more friendly the last few days. He had taken to dropping by the office on the slimmest of pretexts, and telling me how nice I looked if we met by the lifts.

It was all very confusing. Everything was changing so quickly I didn't know what to think any more.

I should be excited. I knew that. In a few months' time I could be back with Jonathan and working with the Chief Executive—and Phin… Well, this had only ever been meant as a temporary exercise anyway. Phin would move on. He'd go back to making television programmes and I wouldn't see him any more. There would be no more jitteriness, no more exasperation, no more teasing. No more doughnuts. And that would be fine, I told myself. It would all work out perfectly.

But there was a sick feeling in the pit of my stomach all the same.

'What's up?' said Phin, when I took in his coffee. It was uncanny the way he always knew if something had happened, no matter how smooth I made my expression.

So I told him what Monique had said. 'Typical Lex,' was his comment, when he heard about his brother's response to the news that his PA was having a much longed for baby. 'He's got no idea. You'd think he could be happy for her before he thought about how her pregnancy will affect Gibson & Grieve!'

'Monique doesn't really mind,' I said, a little uncomfortably. 'She knows what he's like. The normal rules don't apply to someone like Lex.'

'Well, they should,' said Phin. He was leaning back, twirling a pen between his fingers. 'So what about you?' he asked, blue eyes suddenly intent. 'Do you really want to work for a man who wouldn't know what a doughnut was, let alone think about buying you one?'

'It would be a good career opportunity for me.' Unable to bear it any longer, I held out my hand for the pen, and after a stubborn moment he surrendered it, dropping it into my open palm.

'At least I wouldn't have to put up with your endless fiddling any longer,' I said, putting the pen back into its holder. 'And it might be easier when our supposed romance falls through,' I added. 'It would look a bit odd if we carried on working together perfectly happily when…if…'

'When you're back with Jonathan?' Phin finished for me.

There was an unusual note in his voice that made me look sharply at him.

'Even if that doesn't happen, we can't carry on like this indefinitely,' I pointed out.

'Then we'll have to make sure it does happen,' he said, swinging his feet off the desk abruptly. 'Maybe it's time to intensify our campaign. When's the launch party for the *Charmless Chef*?'

The *Charmless Chef* was Phin's own title for a series of TV food programmes that Gibson & Grieve were sponsoring that spring. It was actually called *Hodge Hits*, after the presenter, celebrity chef Stephen Hodge. Hodge was famously rude, and prone to the most appalling temper tantrums. Very early in his career he had discovered that the worse he behaved, the more audiences would want to watch him and the more he would be paid.

This meant Gibson & Grieve would get even more publicity from their sponsorship of the programme, and a fabulous party had been planned to mark the launch and appease his monstrous ego. All senior staff were on a three line whip to turn up and do whatever it took to keep Stephen Hodge happy. Except Lex, of course. He hated socialising, and only went out when absolutely necessary. On this occasion Phin was lined up to represent him and make a speech.

'It's on Friday,' I said.

'Jonathan will be there, won't he?'

'Of course. He negotiated the deal with Stephen Hodge,' I reminded Phin.

'In that case you'll have to pull out all the stops. You always look smart, but on Friday you've got to look stunning. Take tomorrow off and buy a special dress if you have to, but wear something that will knock Jonathan's socks off.'

'He'll be too busy with Stephen Hodge to notice me,' I protested, but Phin refused to listen to any objections.

'If you get the right dress he'll notice you, all right,' he said. 'Besides, I have a cunning plan up my sleeve to relax you.'

'What sort of plan?' I asked suspiciously. I had tried to loosen up whenever we'd been out together, but it was almost impossible when every cell in my body jolted if Phin so much as grazed me with his touch.

'I'll explain on Friday,' he said. 'The launch is at seven, isn't it? We might as well go straight from here.'

Which is how I ended up changing in the directors' bathroom that Friday evening. I'd brought my dress in on a hanger, and carried shoes and make-up in a separate bag.

I had put the need to look stunning to Anne, who had borne me off late-night shopping the night before, and bullied me into buying the most expensive dress I'd ever owned. Even though I felt faintly sick whenever I thought about my credit card bill, I couldn't regret it. It was *so* beautiful.

I don't really know how to begin to describe it. It was red, but not that hard pillarbox red that's so hard to wear. This was a softer, deeper, warmer red—a simple sleeveless sheath, with a layer of chiffon that floated and swirled as I walked. I wasn't used to such a plunging neckline, and with bare shoulders and a bare back I felt a lot more exposed than usual, but it was the kind of dress you couldn't help but feel good in.

I'd painted my toenails a lovely deep red—Ruby, Ruby—to match my fingers, and slipped my feet into beautiful jewelled sandals. My hair was swept up into a clip, and I thought it looked elegant like that, but I hesitated as I studied my reflection, remembering Phin's librarian comment. On an impulse I pulled the clip out and shook my hair free, and then I walked back into the office before I could change my mind.

Phin was there, adjusting his bow tie, but his fingers froze when he saw me. There was a moment of stunned silence. 'Dear God,' he said blankly.

My confidence promptly evaporated. 'What's wrong with it?' I asked, looking down at my lovely dress. I'd been so sure he would like it.

'Nothing's wrong.' Phin cleared his throat. 'Nothing at all. You look…incredible.'

He sounded a bit odd, I thought, but he had said I looked incredible. 'Shall I order a taxi?' I asked after a moment.

'No, it's all sorted,' he said, still distracted. 'A car's waiting downstairs.'

'Oh. Well, shall we go, then?'

Phin seemed to pull himself together. 'Not quite yet, CP,' he said, making a good recovery. 'We need to put my cunning plan into action first.'

'CP?' I echoed blankly.

'Cream…' He waited expectantly for me to supply the rest.

Puff, in fact. I sighed.

'Oh, for heaven's sake,' I said crossly. 'Will you *stop* with the silly names? Now, what *is* this plan of yours?'

'It's really quite simple,' said Phin, coming towards me. 'I'm going to kiss you.'

CHAPTER EIGHT

'Kiss me?' The world titled disconcertingly beneath my feet, and it took me a moment to realise that the air was leaking out of my lungs. I drew in a hissing breath, glad of the steadying effect of the oxygen. We had been through this before, I remembered. 'What kind of plan is that?'

'A good one,' said Phin.

'We agreed that you would only kiss me again if it was necessary,' I reminded him, backing away. My voice was embarrassingly croaky, but under the circumstances—i.e. pounding heart, racing pulse, entrails squeezed with nerves or, more worryingly, anticipation—I didn't think I did too badly.

'I think it *is* necessary,' he said.

I had ended up against the desk, the wood digging into the back of my thighs. 'There's no one else here,' I pointed out bravely. 'How can it be necessary?'

Phin kept coming until he was right in front of me. 'That's the whole point,' he said.

'I've been thinking about it. If we kiss before we go out every time you'll get used to it. It'll just seem part of the evening, like putting on your lipstick—although you might think about doing that *after* we kiss next time. You'll look much more relaxed after a kiss,' he went on. 'Remember how well it worked before the *Glitz* interview?'

'We're not kissing like that again!' My eyes went involuntarily to the sofas on the other side of the room. If we ended up on one of those we'd never get to the party.

'Maybe not *quite* like that,' Phin agreed. A smile hovered around his mouth. The mouth I was doing my level best not to look at. 'Not that it wasn't very nice, but what we want now is for you to feel more comfortable. Once kissing me feels normal, you'll stop feeling so tense whenever I touch you.'

'It's not going to feel normal tonight.'

'No, but I can tell you that if you go to the

party in that dress, looking thoroughly kissed, it won't just be Jonathan I'll be fighting off with a stick,' Phin promised.

Jonathan. The thought of him steadied me. Jonathan was the reason I was wearing this dress…wasn't he?

'Go on, admit it,' said Phin. 'It's a good plan, isn't it?'

I eyed him dubiously. I couldn't help remembering the last time we had kissed. I had got carried away then, and I didn't want that to happen again. On the other hand, I didn't want to admit to Phin that I was nervous about losing control. Somehow I had to pretend that it wasn't that big a deal.

'It might work,' I conceded, and he grinned.

'Come along, then—pucker up, cream puff,' he said. 'The sooner we get it over with, the sooner we can get to the party.'

'Oh, very well.' I gave in. 'If you really think it'll help.'

Maybe it *would* help, I told myself. Instead of constantly wondering what it would be like to touch him again, I would know.

So I stood very still and lifted my face for Phin's kiss, pursing my lips and closing my eyes.

And willing myself not to respond.

Nothing happened at first, and, feeling foolish, I opened my eyes again in time to see him brush my hair gently back over my shoulders. Then very slowly, almost thoughtfully, he slid his hands up the sides of my throat to cup my face. His eyes never left mine, and I felt as if I were trapped in their blueness. My heart was slamming against my ribs.

My mouth felt dry, and I had moistened my lips before I realised what an inviting gesture it was.

Phin smiled. We were so close I could see every eyelash, every one of the tiny creases in his lips, the precise depth of the dent at the corner of his mouth, and I felt dizzy with the nearness of him.

By the time he lowered his head and touched his mouth to mine my blood was thumping with anticipation, and I couldn't help the tiny gasp of relief that parted my lips beneath his.

I willed myself to stay still and unresponsive. All I had to do was stand there for a few seconds and it would be over. How difficult could it be?

You try it. That's all I can say. Try not responding when a man with warm, strong hands twines his fingers in your hair and pulls you closer. When a man with warm, sure lips explores your mouth tantalisingly gently at first, then more insistently. When he smells wonderful and tastes better.

When every kiss pulls at a thread inside you, unravelling you faster and faster, until the world rocks and your bones melt and the only way to stay upright is to clutch at him and kiss him back.

'That's better,' murmured Phin when he lifted his head at last.

I was flushed and trembling, but I was glad to see that his breathing wasn't quite steady either.

'There—it wasn't so bad, was it?' he added, sliding his hands reluctantly from my hair.

'It was fine,' I managed, hoping my legs were going to hold me up without him to hang on to. I was very glad there was a car waiting downstairs. It was going to take all I had to get to the lift, and I was in no shape to trek to the tube— even if my shoes had been up to it.

For reasons best known to the television company, the launch party for *Hodge Hits* was being held in the Orangery at Kew Gardens. I'd never been before, and it looked so beautiful with that row of high arched windows that I actually forgot my throbbing lips and crackling pulse as I looked around me.

The room was already crowded, but I caught a glimpse of Stephen Hodge, surrounded by groupies as always, wearing his trademark scowl. He had long hair that always looked as if it could do with a good wash, and he was very thin. There's something unnatural about a thin chef, don't you think? I suspected that Stephen Hodge never ate his own food and, having seen some of his more innovative recipes, I didn't blame him.

'Now, be nice,' said Phin, seeing my lip curl.

'That's good, coming from you,' I countered. 'Are you sure you've got the right speech with you?'

He'd tried a scurrilous version on me earlier, which had been very funny but which was unlikely to go down well with either Hodge or Jonathan, who had been instrumental in setting up the sponsorship. I was hoping that he had a suitably bland alternative in his pocket some-where, but with Phin you never knew.

'Don't worry, I've got the toadying version right here,' he said, patting his jacket. 'Besides, you're not in PA mode tonight. You're my incredibly sexy girlfriend and don't you forget it. Talking of which—' he nudged me '—look who's heading our way. Or rather don't look. You're supposed to be absorbed in me.'

I risked a swift glance anyway, and spotted Jonathan, pushing his way through the crowd towards us. He had Lori with him, looking tiny and delicate in a sophisticated ivory number. I immediately felt crass and garish in comparison, but it was too late to run away.

'Remember—make him jealous,' Phin murmured in my ear.

There was no way Jonathan would even notice me next to Lori, I thought, but I turned obediently and slid my arm around Phin's waist, snuggling closer and smiling up at him as if I hadn't noticed Jonathan at all.

Perhaps that kiss had worked after all. It felt oddly comfortable to be leaning against Phin's hard, solid body—so much so, in fact, that when Jonathan's voice spoke behind me I was genuinely startled.

'I'm glad you're here, Phin,' Jonathan began. 'I just wanted to check everything's under control. We want to kick off with your speech, and then Stephen's going to—'

He broke off as his gaze fell on me, and I gave him my most dazzling smile. 'Summer!'

'Hi, Jonathan,' I said.

Gratifyingly, he looked pole-axed. 'I didn't recognise you,' he said.

Beside him, Lori raised elegant brows. 'Nor did I. That colour really suits you, Summer.'

'Thank you,' I said coolly. 'You look great, too.'

Jonathan was still watching me with a stunned expression. Funny, I had dreamt of him looking at me just that way, but now that he was doing it I felt awkward and embarrassed.

'You look amazing tonight,' he said, and all I could think was that it wasn't fair of him to be talking to me like that when Lori was standing right beside him.

'Doesn't she?' Phin locked gazes with Jonathan in an unspoken challenge, and slid his hand possessively beneath my hair to rest it on the nape of my neck.

I could feel the warm weight of it—not

pressing uncomfortably, but just there, a reassuring connection—and I had one of those weird out of body moments when you can look at yourself as if from the outside. I could see how easy we looked together, how right.

Jonathan and Lori had no reason not to believe that we were a real couple. They would look at us and assume that we were used to touching intimately, to understanding each other completely. To not knowing precisely where one finished and the other began, so that there was no more me, no more Phin, just an us.

The thought of an 'us' made the world tip a little. Abruptly I was back in my body, and desperately aware of Phin's solid strength beneath my arm, of the tingling imprint of his palm on my neck.

There *was* no us, I had to remind myself. I only just stopped myself shaking my head to clear it. Everything about the party seemed so unreal, but I was bizarrely able to carry on a conversation with Jonathan and Lori while every cell in my body was straining with Phin's closeness.

True, it wasn't much of a conversation. Some

small talk about Stephen Hodge and his vile temper. I complimented Lori on her earrings, she mentioned my shoes, but all I could really think about was the way Phin was absently stroking my neck, his thumb caressing my skin.

Every graze of his fingertips stoked the sizzle deep inside me, and I was alarmingly aware that it could crackle into life at any time. If I wasn't careful there would be a *whoosh* and I would spontaneously combust. That would spoil Stephen Hodge's party all right.

I had to move away from Phin or it would all get very messy. Straightening, I made a show of pushing my hair behind my ears. 'Um…isn't it time for your speech?' I asked him with an edge of desperation.

'I suppose I'd better throw a few scraps to the monster's ego,' sighed Phin. 'He hasn't been kow-towed to for all of thirty seconds! Where would you like me to do it, Jonathan?'

'We've set up a podium,' said Jonathan. 'I'd better go and warn Stephen that we're ready to go.'

'Lead on,' said Phin, and held out his hand to me. 'Are you coming, CP?'

Jonathan looked puzzled. 'CP?'

I smiled uncomfortably as I took Phin's hand. 'Private joke,' I said.

After that, we had to kiss every time we got ready to go out. 'Come here and be kissed,' Phin would say, holding out his arms. 'This is the best part of the day.'

I was very careful to keep reminding myself that those kisses didn't mean a thing, but secretly I found myself looking forward to them. I always tried to make a joke of it, of course.

'Oh, let's get it over with, then,' I'd say, putting my arms briskly around his neck, but there was always a moment when our determined jokiness faded into something else entirely, something warm and yearning—the moment when I succumbed to the honeyed pleasure spilling along my veins, to the tug of longing and the wicked crackle of excitement between us.

I would like to say that it was me who put an end to the kiss every time, but I'd be lying. It was almost always Phin who lifted his head before I remembered that it was only supposed to be a quick kiss and thought about pulling away.

'We're getting good at this now,' Phin would

say. I noticed, though, that the famous smile looked a little forced, and he was often distracted afterwards.

The theory had been that the more we kissed, the easier it would get. But it didn't work like that. It got more and more difficult to disentangle those kisses from reality, harder and harder to remember that I wanted Jonathan, that Phin was just amusing himself.

To remember why we had to stop at a kiss.

And the worst thing was that there was a bit of me that didn't want to.

Whenever I realised that I'd give myself a stern ticking off. This would involve a rigorous reminder of all the reasons why it would be stupid to fall for someone like Phin. He wasn't serious. He wasn't steady. He didn't want to settle down. I'd end up hurt and humiliated and I'd have no one to blame but myself.

Much—*much*—more sensible to remember why I had loved Jonathan. Why I *still* loved him, I'd have to correct myself an alarming number of times.

Jonathan was everything Phin wasn't. He was everything I needed.

I just couldn't always remember why.

Ironically, the harder I tried to remind myself of how much I wanted Jonathan, the more often Jonathan found excuses to drop into the office.

'You can't tell me our plan's not working now,' Phin said to me one evening as we sipped champagne at some gallery opening. 'Jonathan's always sniffing around nowadays. I trip over him every time I come into office. I notice he was there again this afternoon.'

He sounded uncharacteristically morose, and I shot him a curious look.

'He just came to see what I knew about the Cameroon trip,' I said uncomfortably, although I had no idea why I felt suddenly guilty.

'Ha!' said Phin mirthlessly. 'Was that all he could think of as an excuse?'

'It wasn't an excuse,' I said.

I had the feeling Jonathan was looking forward to going to Africa about as much as I was. I'd tried everything I could to get out of the trip, but Phin was adamant. The flights were booked for the end of March, and I was dreading it.

It was so *not* my kind of travelling. I like city breaks—Paris or Rome or New York—and hotels with hairdryers and mini bars, all of which were obviously going to be in short supply on the Cameroon trip. We'd had to be vaccinated against all sorts of horrible tropical diseases, and Phin had presented us all with a kit list so that we'd know what to take with us. Hairdryers didn't appear on it. I would be taking a rucksack instead of a pull-along case, walking boots in place of smart city shoes.

'And don't bother with any make-up,' Phin had told me. 'Sunblock is all you'll need.'

I was taking some anyway.

I don't suppose Jonathan was bothered about the make-up issue, but he was clearly anxious about the whole experience. Phin had presented the trip as a staff development exercise, and I suspected Jonathan didn't want to be developed any more than I did.

'I'm really glad you're going to be in same group when we go to Africa,' he had said to me, only that afternoon.

Phin was eyeing me moodily over the rim of his champagne glass. 'Nobody could be *that* worried about going to Africa. He just wants to hang around and talk to you.' He scowled at me.

'I hope you're not going to give in too easily. Make him work to get you back!'

'Look, what's the problem?' I demanded. 'Isn't the whole idea that Jonathan starts to find me interesting again? Or did you want to spend the rest of your life stuck in this pretence?'

'It just irritates me that he's being so cautious.' Phin hunched a shoulder. 'If you'd been mine, and I'd realised what an idiot I'd been, I wouldn't be dithering around talking about malaria pills, or whether to pack an extra towel, and how many pairs of socks to take. I'd be sweeping you off your feet.'

It wasn't like Phin to be grouchy. That was *my* role. The worst thing was that there was a bit of me that agreed with him. But I had no intention of admitting *that*.

'Yes, well, the whole point is that you're *not* Jonathan,' I said. 'Yes, he's being careful—but that's only sensible. As far as he knows I'm in love with his boss. It would be madness to charge in and try and sweep me off unless he was sure how I felt.'

I lifted my chin. 'And I wouldn't *want* to be with someone that reckless,' I went on. 'I'd rather have someone who thought things through, who saw how the land lay, and then acted when he was sure of success. Someone like Jonathan, in fact.'

And right then I even believed it.

Or told myself I did, anyway.

Now, I know what you're thinking, but you have to remember how clear Phin always made it that he would never consider a permanent relationship. He liked teasing me, he liked kissing me, and we got on surprisingly well, but there was never any question that there might be more than that.

I'm not a fool. I knew just how easy it would be to fall in love with him. But I knew, too, how pointless it would be. I might grumble about him endlessly, but it was fun being with Phin. Much to my own surprise, I was enjoying our pretend affair.

But I wouldn't let myself lose sight of the fact that the security I craved lay elsewhere. I was earning better money now, and could start to think about buying a flat. Lori, I'd heard, was back with her old boyfriend and, whatever I might say to Phin, I knew Jonathan was definitely showing signs of renewed interest in me. Somewhere along the line I'd lost my desperate adoration of him, but he was still attractive, still nice, still steady. I could feel safe with Jonathan, I knew.

I had never had a better chance to have everything I wanted, and I wasn't going to throw it away—no matter how good it felt being with Phin.

I had run out of excuses. Hunched and sullen, I sat in the departure lounge at Heathrow, nursing a beaker of tea. It was five-thirty in the morning, and I didn't want to be there. I wanted to be at home, in bed, soon to begin my nice, safe routine.

I did the same thing every day. I woke up at half past six and made myself a cup of tea. Then I showered, dried my hair and put on my make-up. I took the same bus, the same tube, and stopped at Otto's at the same time to buy a cappuccino from Lucia.

You could set your watch by the time I got to the office and sat down behind my immaculately tidy desk. Then I'd sit there and savour the feeling of everything being in its place and under control, which lasted only until Phin appeared and stirred up the air and made the whole notion of control a distant memory.

'It's a rut,' Phin had said when I told him about my routine.

'You're missing the point. I *like* my rut.'

'Trust me, you're going to like Africa, too.'

'I'm not,' I said sulkily. 'I'm going to hate every minute of it.'

And at first I did.

We had to change planes, and after what seemed like hours hanging around in airports it was dark by the time we arrived at Douala. The airport there was everything I had feared. It was hot, crowded, shambolic. There seemed to be a lot of shouting.

I shrank into Phin as we pushed our way through the press of people and outside, to where a minibus was supposed to be waiting but wasn't. The tropical heat was suffocating, and the smell of airport fuel mingled with sweat and unfinished concrete lodged somewhere at the back of my throat.

Through it all I was very aware of Phin, steady and good-humoured, bantering in French with the customs officials who wanted to open every single one of our bags. He was wearing jungle trousers and an olive-green shirt, and amazingly managed to look cool and unfazed—while my hair was sticking to my head and I could feel the perspiration trickling down my back.

There were twelve of us in our group. Hand-picked by Phin, together we represented a cross-section of the headquarters staff, from secretaries like me to security staff, executives to cleaners. I knew most of the others by sight, and Phin had assured us we would be a close-knit team by the time we returned ten days later. I could tell we were bonding already in mutual unease at the airport.

'Everything's fine,' Phin said soothingly as we all fretted about the non-appearance of the mini-bus. 'It'll be here in a minute.'

The minute stretched to twenty, but eventually a rickety mini-bus did indeed turn up. It took us to a strange hotel where we slept four to a room under darned mosquito nets. There were tiny translucent geckos on the walls, and a rattling air-conditioning unit kept me awake all night. Oh, yes, and I found a cockroach in the shower.

'Tell me again why I'm supposed to love all

this,' I grumbled to Phin the next morning. I was squeezed between him and the driver in the front of a Jeep that bounced over potholes and swerved around the dogs and goats that wandered along the road with a reckless disregard for my stomach, not to mention any oncoming traffic.

'Look at the light,' Phin answered. To my relief we had slowed to crawl through a crowded market. 'Look at how vibrant the colours are. Look at that girl's smile.' He gestured at the stalls lining the road. 'Look at those bananas, those tomatoes, those pineapples! Nothing's wrapped in plastic, or flown thousands of miles so that it loses its taste.'

His arm lay behind my head along the back of the seat, and he turned to look down into my face. 'Listen to the music coming out of the shops. Doesn't it make you want to get out and dance? How can you *not* love it?'

'It just comes naturally to me,' I muttered.

'And you're with me,' he pointed out, careless of our colleagues in the back seat.

I was very aware of them—although I couldn't imagine they would be able to hear much over the sound of the engine, the music spilling out of the shacks on either side of the road and the children running after us shouting, 'Happy! Happy! Happy!'

'We're together on an adventure,' said Phin. 'What more could you want?'

I sighed. 'I don't know where to begin answering that!'

'Oh, come on, Summer. This is fun.'

'You sound just like my mother,' I said sourly. 'This reminds me of the way Mum would drag me around the country, telling me how much I should be loving it, when all I wanted was to stay at home.'

'Maybe she knew that you had the capacity to love it all if only you'd let yourself,' said Phin. 'Maybe she was like me and thought you were afraid of how much love and passion was locked up inside you.'

It certainly sounded like the kind of thing my mother *would* think.

'Why do you care?' Cross, I lowered my voice and looked straight ahead, just in case anyone behind was listening or had omitted to put lip-reading skills on their CV. 'We don't have a real relationship, and even if we did it would only be temporary. You can't tell me you'd be hanging around long enough to care about my *capacity* for anything.'

There was a pause. 'I hate waste,' said Phin at last.

I had thought the road from Douala was bad, but I had no idea then of what lay ahead.

After that little town, the road deteriorated until there wasn't even an attempt at tarmac, and a downpour didn't exactly improve matters. Our little convoy of Jeeps lurched for hours over tracks through slippery red mud. We had to stop several times to push one or other of the vehicles out of deep ruts gouged out by trucks.

'This is what it's like trying to get *you* out of your rut,' Phin said to me with a grin, as we put our shoulders to the back of our Jeep once more. His face was splattered with mud from the spinning tyres, and I didn't want to think about what I looked like. I could feel the sprayed mud drying on my skin like a measles rash.

'Of course it's harder in your case,' he went on. 'Not so muddy, though.'

We were all filthy by the time we reached

Aduaba—a village wedged between a broad brown river and the dark green press of the rainforest. There was a cluster of huts, with mud daub walls and roofs thatched with palm leaves, or occasionally a piece of corrugated iron, and what seemed like hundreds of children splashing in the water.

My relief at getting out of the Jeep soon turned to horror when I discovered that the huts represented luxury accommodation compared to what we were getting: a few pieces of tarpaulin thrown over a makeshift frame to provide shelter.

'I'm so far out of my comfort zone I don't know what to say,' I told Phin.

'Oh, come now—it's not that bad,' he said, but I could tell that he was enjoying my dismay. 'It's not as if it's cold, and the tarpaulin will keep you dry.'

'But where are we going to sleep?'

'Why do you think I made you buy a sleeping mat?'

'We're sleeping on the *ground*?'

His smile was answer enough.

I looked at him suspiciously. 'What about you?'

'I'll be right here with you—and everyone else, before you get in a panic.'

I opened my mouth, then closed it again. 'Does Lex know the conditions here?' I demanded. I couldn't believe he would have put his staff through this if he'd had any idea of what it would be like.

'I shouldn't think so,' said Phin cheerfully. 'The conditions aren't bad, Summer,' he went on more seriously. 'This isn't meant to be a five star jolly. It's *meant* to be challenging. It's all about pushing you all out of your comfort zones and seeing what you're made of. It's about giving you a brief glimpse of another community and thinking about the ways staff and customers at Gibson & Grieve can make a connection with them.'

I set my jaw stubbornly, and he shook his head with a grin. 'I bet,' he said, 'that you'll end up enjoying this much more than going to some polo match, or having a corporate box at the races, or whatever Lex usually does to keep staff happy.'

'A bet?' I folded my arms. 'How much?'

'You want to take me on?'

'I do,' I said. 'If I win, you have to…'

I tried to think about what would push Phin out

of *his* comfort zone. I could hardly suggest he settled down and got married, but there was no reason he shouldn't commit to something.

'…you have to agree to get to work by nine every day for as long as we're working together,' I decided.

Phin whistled. 'High stakes. And if I win?'

'Well, I think that's academic, but you choose.'

'That's very rash of you, cream puff! Now, let's see…' He tapped his teeth, pretending to ponder a suitable stake. 'Since I know I'm going to win, I'd be a fool not to indulge a little fantasy, wouldn't I?'

'What sort of fantasy?' I asked a little warily.

'Do you care?' he countered. 'I thought you were sure you weren't going to enjoy yourself?'

I looked at the tarpaulin and remembered how thin my sleeping mat had looked. There was no way Phin would win this bet.

'I am sure,' I said. 'Go on—tell me this fantasy of yours.'

'We're at work,' he told me, his eyes glinting with amusement and something else. 'You come into my office with your notebook, and you're wearing one of those prim little suits of yours, and your hair is tied up neatly, and you're wearing your stern glasses.'

'It doesn't sound much of a fantasy to me,' I said. 'That's just normal.'

'Ah, yes, but when you've finished taking notes you don't do what you normally do. You take off your glasses, the way you do, but instead of going back to your desk in my fantasy you come round until you're standing really close to me.'

His voice dropped. 'Then you shake out your hair and you unbutton your jacket *ve-r-ry* slowly and you don't take your eyes off mine the whole time.'

My heart was beating uncomfortably at the picture, but I managed a very creditable roll of my eyes.

'It's a bit hackneyed, isn't it? I was expecting you to come up with something a little more exciting than that.'

The corner of Phin's mouth twitched. 'Well, I *could* make it more exciting, of course, but it wouldn't be fair, given that you're going to have to actually do this.'

'I don't think so,' I said, a combative glint in

my own eyes. Still, there was no point in pushing it. 'So that's it? Take my hair down and unbutton my jacket if—and that's a very big *if*—I enjoy the next ten days?'

'Oh, you would have to kiss me as well,' said Phin. 'As to what happens after the kiss…well, that would be up to you. But it might depend on how many other people were around.'

'I'm sure that wouldn't be a problem,' I said with a confident toss of my head. 'So: hair, jacket, kiss for me if you win, and turning up on time for you if I do? I hope you've got a good alarm clock! This is one bet I'm deadly sure I'm going to win.'

CHAPTER NINE

BUT I lost.

The first night was really uncomfortable, yes, but in the days that followed I was so tired that my sleeping mat might as well have been a feather bed, I slept so soundly.

We spent the next ten days helping the villagers to finish the medical centre they had started a couple of years earlier but had had to abandon when they ran out of money to buy the materials. Somehow Phin had organised delivery of everything that was needed, and I didn't need to be there long to realise what an achievement that was.

It was an eye-opening time for me in more ways than one. For most of the time it was hard, physical labour. It was hot and incredibly humid, and the closest I got to a shower was a dip in the river, but I liked seeing the building take shape. Every day we could stand back and see the results of our labours, and we forgot that our hands were dirty, our nails broken, our hair tangled.

When I think back to that time what I remember most is the laughter. Children laughing, women laughing, everyone laughing together. I'd never met a community that found so much humour in their everyday lives. The people of Aduaba humbled me with their openness, their friendliness and their hospitality, and I cringed when I remembered how dismissive I had been of their huts when I first arrived. When I was invited inside, I found that the mud floors were swept and everything was scrupulously clean and neat.

'Why can't you keep your house like this?' I asked Phin.

The women particularly were hard-working and funny. A few of them had some words of English or French, and I learnt some words of their language. We managed to communicate well enough. I kept my hair tied back, as that was only practical, but I forgot about mascara and lipstick, and it wasn't long before I started to feel the tension that was so familiar to me I barely noticed it most of the time slowly unravelling.

I learnt to appreciate the smell of the rainforest, the way the darkness dropped like a blanket, the beauty of the early-morning mist on the river. I began to listen for the sounds which had seemed so alien at first: the screech of a monkey, the rasp of insects in the dark, the creak and rustle of vegetation, the crash of tropical rain on the tarpaulin and the slow, steady drip of the leaves afterwards.

But most of all my eyes were opened to Phin. It was a long time since I had been able to think of him as no more than a bland celebrity, but I hadn't realised how much more there was to him. He was in his element in Aduaba. He belonged there in a way he never would in the confines of the office.

Wherever there was laughter, I would find him. He spoke much more of the language, and had an extraordinary ability to defuse tension and get everyone working together, sorting out administrative muddles with endless patience. I suppose I hadn't realised how *competent* he was.

I remember watching him out of the corner of my eye as he hammered in a roof joist. His expression was focused, but when one of the other men on the roof shouted what sounded like a curse he glanced up and shouted something back that made them all laugh. I saw the familiar smile light up his face and felt something that wasn't familiar at all twist and unlock inside me.

At night I was desperately aware of him breathing nearby, and knew that he was the reason I wasn't afraid. He was the reason I was here at all.

He was the reason I was changing.

And I *was* changing. I could feel it. I felt like a butterfly struggling out of its chrysalis, hardly able to believe what was happening to me.

That I was enjoying it.

It wasn't all work. I played on the beach with the children, and helped the women cook. One of the men took us into the forest and showed us a bird spider on its web. I kid you not, that spider was as big as my hand. None of us thought of wandering off on our own after that.

Once Jonathan and I took a little boat with an outboard motor and puttered down the river. I felt quite comfortable with him by then. My mind was full of Aduaba and our life there, and I'd almost forgotten the desperate yearning I had once felt for him.

We drifted in companionable silence for a while. 'It's funny to think we'll be going home soon,' said Jonathan at last. 'I'll admit I was dreading this trip, but it's been one of the best things I've ever done.'

'I feel that, too.'

'It's made me realise that I never really knew you before, when we…you know…' He petered off awkwardly.

'I know,' I said, trailing my fingers in the water. 'But I think I've changed since I've been here. I wasn't like this before, or if I was I didn't know it. I thought I was going to hate it but I don't.' I remembered my bet with Phin and shivered a little.

'I know you and Phin are good together,' Jonathan blurted suddenly, 'but I just want you to know that I think you're wonderful, Summer, and if you ever change your mind about Phin I'd like another chance.'

I stilled for a moment. How many times had I dreamt of Jonathan saying those words? Now that he had, I didn't know what to say.

I pulled my hand out of the water. 'What about Lori?' I asked. It wasn't that long since he'd been mad about her.

'Lori's back with her ex. It was quite intense for a while, but I think I always knew she was on the rebound, and now that she's back with him I realise how close I came to making a big mistake.'

So I couldn't use Lori as an excuse to say no, I thought, and then caught myself up. Excuse? What do you need an excuse for, Summer?

'I know I didn't appreciate you when I had you, but I can see now that you were so much better for me than Lori,' Jonathan was saying. 'We've got so much more in common.'

'Yes, I suppose we have,' I said slowly.

He leant forward eagerly. 'We've got the same outlook, the same values.'

It was true. That was exactly what I had loved about him, but why did he have to wait until now to realise it? Frankly, his timing sucked.

'Jonathan, I—'

'It's OK,' he interrupted me. 'You don't need to say anything. I know how things are with you and Phin right now. I just wanted to tell you how I felt—to let you know that I'm always here for you.'

Why did he have to be so nice? I thought

crossly as we made our way back. It would have been so much easier for me if he had turned out to be lazy, or a whinger, or even if he just hadn't liked Cameroon very much. Then I could have decided that I didn't love him after all. But in lots of ways I had never liked Jonathan as much as I did then.

Jonathan knew Phin's reputation as well as I did. He wouldn't have said anything if he hadn't thought there was a good chance that my supposed relationship with Phin would end sooner or later.

As it would.

Everything was working out just as Phin had said. It was just a pity I didn't know what I really wanted any more.

There was a party on our last night in Aduaba. We drank palm wine in the hot, tropical night and listened to the sounds of the forest for the last time. Then the music started. There's an ir-resistible rhythm to African music. I could feel it beating in my blood, and when the women pulled me to my feet I danced with them.

I must have looked ridiculous, stamping my feet and waggling my puny bottom, but I didn't care. The only time I faltered was when I caught Phin watching me, with such a blaze of expression in his eyes that I stumbled momentarily. But when I looked again he was laughing and allowing himself to be drawn into the dance and I decided I must have imagined it.

I ran my fingers over my keyboard as if I had never seen one before. It felt very strange to be back in the office. My head was still full of Africa, and I had found the tube stifling and oppressive on my way into work that morning.

Unsettled, I switched on my computer, and sat down to scroll through the hundreds of e-mails that had accumulated while we'd been away. It was hard to focus, though, and my mind kept drifting back to Aduaba and Phin.

Phin stripped to the waist like the other men, his muscles bulging with effort as they lifted the heavy timbers into place.

Phin laughing with the children in the river.

Phin looking utterly at ease in the heat and the humidity and the wildness.

He strolled in some time after ten, and all the air evaporated from my lungs at the sight of him.

I was annoyed to see that he seemed just the same as always, while I felt completely different.

I looked at him over the top of my glasses. 'I see you didn't invest in that alarm clock,' I said crisply, to cover the fact that my heart was cantering around my chest in an alarmingly uncontrolled way.

'No, but then I don't need to turn up on time every day, do I?' said Phin, not at all put out by the sharpness of my greeting. '*I'm* not the one who lost the bet.'

The mention of the bet silenced me, and I bit my lip. Nothing more had been said about it, and I'd convinced myself that Phin hadn't really been serious. It had just been joke...hadn't it?

Much to my relief, Phin didn't say any more, but went into his office and threw himself into his chair. 'So, what's been happening?' he asked. 'Is there anything that needs to be dealt with right away?'

Grateful to him for behaving normally, I took in my notebook and ran through the most urgent issues. 'Shall I make some coffee?' I said, when I had finished scribbling notes.

'Not just yet,' said Phin. 'There's the small matter of the bet we made.' He smiled at me as I stared at him in consternation. 'I think you owe me.'

It was typical of him to let me relax and then catch me off guard. I should have known he'd do something like that.

I swallowed. 'Now?'

'I always think it's best to pay debts straight away, don't you? Do you remember the terms?'

Drawing a breath, I took off my glasses. 'I think so,' I said.

Now that it had come to it, I felt a flicker of excitement. I met Phin's eyes and wondered if he was waiting for me to renegotiate, and I knew suddenly that I didn't want to do that.

'You were right,' I said clearly. 'I loved it.'

Calmly, I got to my feet and went round the desk to where Phin sat in a high-backed executive chair. He was silent, watching me as I leant back against the desk and very deliberately pulled the clip from my hair, so that I could shake it loose and let it tumble around my face.

How embarrassing, my sensible side was saying. How unbelievably inappropriate. How *tacky*.

It was bad enough making a bet like that with your boss, without playing up to his patriarchal male fantasies. How had I got myself into a situation where I was feeling a bit naughty, a bit dirty, a bit sexy *in the office*?

How could I possibly be turned on by it?

But I was. I can hardly bear to remember it without cringing, but at the time…oh, yes, I certainly was.

I smiled slowly at Phin. 'How am I doing so far?'

'Perfect,' he said, but his voice was strained and I felt a spurt of triumph, even power that I could have that effect on him just by letting down my hair.

Levering myself away from the desk, I moved closer to him. One by one I undid the buttons of my jacket, even though I was having one of those out-of-body experiences again and screaming at myself, *What are you doing? Stop it right now!*

Phin said nothing, but his eyes were very dark as he watched me, and I could see him struggling to keep his breathing even. When my jacket was open to reveal the cream silk camisole I wore underneath, I leant down and pressed my mouth to the pulse that was beating frantically in his throat.

I heard Phin suck in his breath, and I smiled against his skin, slipping my arms around his neck and easing myself onto his lap so that I could kiss my way slowly, slowly, along his jaw to the edge of his mouth.

'Am I doing it right?' I whispered.

'God, yes,' he said raggedly, and his arms came up to fasten around me as I kissed him at last.

His lips parted beneath mine, drawing me in, and the chair spun round as his hand slid possessively under my skirt. It might have been tacky, it might have been deeply, deeply inappropriate, but it felt so good I didn't care.

I have a hazy memory that I thought I should be in control, but if I ever was I soon lost it. It wasn't as if Phin was in control either. That kiss was stronger than both of us. It ripped through our meagre defences, rampaging like wildfire in the blood, sucking us up like a twister to a place far from the office where there were only lips and tongues, only hands moving greedily, insistently, only the pounding of our hearts and the throb of our bodies and the sweet, dangerous intoxication of a kiss that went on and on and on.

Sadly, the office hadn't forgotten us. The sound of a throat being loudly cleared gradually penetrated. We paused, our mouths still pressed together, our tongues still entwined, and then our eyes opened at exactly the same time.

The throat was cleared again. As if at a trigger, we jerked apart, and I would have leapt off Phin's knee if he hadn't held me tightly in place as he swung his chair back to face the door.

Lex Gibson was standing there, looking bored.

'I did knock,' he said. 'Three times.'

I struggled to get up, but Phin held me tight. 'We're a bit busy here, Lex.'

'So I saw. Good to see that work ethic kicking in at last,' said Lex, who had his own line in sardonic humour when it suited him.

'Did you want something?' Phin countered. 'Or are you just here to ruin a perfect morning?'

'I wouldn't be here if it wasn't important,' said Lex dryly.

That hardly needed saying. Lex rarely left his office. Staff were summoned to see *him*, and could often be seen quailing in Monique's office while they waited their turn. It was unheard of for him to seek someone out himself.

Phin sighed as he released me. 'It had better be,' he said.

My cheeks were burning as I scrambled to my feet, desperately trying to smooth back my hair and rebutton my jacket as I went.

'Um…can I get you some coffee?' I asked Lex. I was mortified at having been caught in such a compromising position but, with that kiss still thrumming through me, probably not nearly as mortified as I should have been. 'Then I can leave you two together.'

'Actually, this concerns you,' he said.

Oh, God, he was going to sack me for unprofessional behaviour!

'Shall we sit down?' said Lex, gesturing at the sofas.

Biting my lip, I sat obediently, and Phin came to join me. We glanced at each other like naughty children, then looked at Lex.

'I believe Monique has already told you that she's expecting a baby?' he began, with a hint of disapproval.

I was so relieved that I wasn't getting fired that I started to smile—before it occurred to me that something might be wrong.

'Yes, she did. Is everything OK?' I asked in concern.

'No. At least, Monique is all right,' he amended. 'But she's been ordered to rest until the baby is born. Something to do with high blood pressure.'

I could tell Lex wasn't up on pregnancy talk. Not that I was much better.

'Oh, dear. Poor Monique. She'll have to be so careful.'

'It's very inconvenient,' said Lex austerely. 'It was bad enough that I was going to lose her in August, but she went home on Friday and now she's not coming in again until after her maternity leave.'

'So why are you here, Lex?' asked Phin with a hint of impatience. 'Or can we guess?'

'I would imagine you could, yes. Obviously I need a PA immediately—and preferably one who's familiar with my office.'

'Summer, in fact.' Phin's voice was flat.

Lex looked at me. 'Monique told me she'd

mentioned the possibility of you replacing her during her maternity leave already. I'd like you to come and work for me now, even if it's only to help me through this immediate period.'

I was finding it difficult to concentrate. I'd been jerked so rudely out of that kiss, and every cell in my body was still screaming with frustration.

'Well…er…what about Phin? I mean… working for Phin,' I stumbled, realising that my concern for Phin might be misinterpreted in view of what Lex had just seen us doing.

'I'm here as a courtesy,' said Lex, looking at his brother. 'I appreciate that you've established a good working relationship with Summer—a little too good, some might say—but your office doesn't generate nearly the same amount of work as yet. It seems to me that you could quite easily manage with another secretary, or share assistance with one of the other directors.'

Phin's jaw tightened. 'I'm not going to get into a discussion about how much work I do or don't do here, Lex,' he said grittily. 'This is about Summer and where she wants to work. I'm sure she's happy to help you over this crisis period…' He looked at me for confirmation and I nodded.

'Of course.'

'But after that it's up to her.'

'That seems fair enough,' said Lex, getting to his feet. 'I'm grateful,' he said to me, and I got up, too.

'Er…would you like me to come now?'

'If you would.'

That was Lex—straight back to work. It clearly didn't occur to him that I might want to talk to Phin on my own.

I glanced at Phin, who was watching me with an unreadable expression. 'I'll…er…I'll speak to you later,' I said awkwardly.

'Sure. Don't let him work you too hard.'

So there I was, walking down the corridor with Lex to the best career opportunity of my life, and all I could think was that only minutes ago I had been in the middle of the best kiss of my life.

Lex behaved as if nothing whatsoever had happened, and I was grateful. I couldn't believe now that I had actually stood there in front of Phin, unbuttoning my jacket, that I had kissed him like that. But at the same time I couldn't believe that I had stopped.

I was torn: my body raging with the aftermath of that kiss, but my mind slowly beginning to clear. Where would it have ended if Lex hadn't interrupted us? Would we really have made love in the office with the door open? I went hot and cold at the thought. I could have jeopardised my whole career. It had been bad enough Lex finding us like that, without the whole office stopping by to gawp at Summer Curtis out of control with her boss.

Everything was getting out of hand, and I didn't like it.

It was a strange, disorientating day. I slipped back into place in Lex's office as if I had never been away. Monique was fantastically efficient, which helped. It meant I could pick up where she had left.

Lotty, the junior secretary who had replaced me, was hugely relieved when I appeared. 'I was terrified I was going to have to take over myself,' she confided. 'I like my job, but Lex Gibson reduces me to a gibbering wreck.'

I knew what that felt like. Phin could do the same to me, but for very different reasons.

Somehow I managed to keep up a calm,

capable front all day, and I don't think anyone guessed that behind my cool façade I was reliving that kiss again and again.

The more I thought about it, the more glad I was that Lex had interrupted us when he had. I mean, that wasn't *me*, sliding seductively onto my boss's lap. I was cool, I was competent, I was *sensible*.

Although it would have been hard to guess that from the way I'd been carrying on recently. It wasn't sensible to get involved with your boss, to pretend a relationship you didn't have, to make stupid bets with him, to *kiss* him. What had I been thinking? I had put my career—everything I believed in, everything I'd always wanted—at risk. I'd done exactly what I had sworn I would never to do and got carried away by the moment.

How my mother would cheer if she knew.

At six o'clock I made my way back down to Phin's office. My desk looked empty and forlorn already. I knocked on his door.

Phin was on one of the sofas, reading a report. He dropped it onto the table when he saw me in the doorway and got to his feet, the first blaze of expression in his eyes quickly shielded. 'Hi.'

'Hi.'

There was an awkward pause.

'So how's it going?' he asked after a moment.

'Fine.'

Had we really kissed earlier? Suddenly we were talking to each other like strangers. I couldn't bear it.

Another silence. I stepped into the room and closed the door behind me.

Phin watched me warily. 'Somehow I get the feeling you're not about to pick up where we left off,' he said.

'No,' I agreed. 'I paid my debt.'

But my heart twisted as I said it. It had been so much more than a jokey kiss to close a bet, and we both knew it.

I went to sit on the other sofa. 'I've decided to take the job with Lex while Monique is away.'

'I thought you would,' said Phin, sitting opposite me.

'It's a fantastic career opportunity for me,' I ploughed on. 'And when I thought about it I could see that it would make it much easier for both of us. It would be awkward to carry on working together now.'

'Now?'

'I think it's time to call an end to our pretence,' I said. 'It's served its purpose.'

Phin sat back and regarded me steadily. 'Has Jonathan come through?'

'We had a talk in Aduaba,' I admitted. 'He said he wanted to try again.'

'And what did you say?'

'I said I'd think about it.'

'I see.'

I bit my lip. 'The *Glitz* article has come out. Even Jewel's given up on you.' I tried to joke. 'There's nothing in it for you any more. We should pretend that it's over now.'

'Is that what you want?'

'To be honest, Phin, I don't know *what* I want at the moment,' I said with a sigh. 'It's all been…'

I tried to think of a way to describe how it had felt, but couldn't do it. 'I'm confused,' I said instead. 'You, Jonathan, Africa, this new job…I don't know what I feel about any of it. I don't know what I'm *doing* any more.'

'You seemed to know exactly what you were doing earlier this morning,' said Phin.

I could feel the colour creeping up my throat. 'I got…carried away,' I said with difficulty. 'I'm sorry.'

'Don't apologise for it,' he said almost angrily. 'Getting carried away isn't always a bad thing, Summer.'

'It is for me.' Restlessly, I got to my feet. Hugging my arms together, I went over to the window and looked down at the commuters streaming towards Charing Cross.

'My mother's spent her whole life being carried away by one thing or another,' I told him. 'I was dragged along in her wake, and all I ever wanted was something to hold onto, somewhere I could stay, somewhere I could call home. That's why my job has always been so important to me. I know it's not a high-flying career, but I like it, and I do it well.'

I turned back to Phin, trying to make him understand. 'This morning…that was so unprofessional. When I saw Lex, I thought he was going to sack me. I wouldn't have blamed him, either.'

'He wouldn't have sacked you. I wouldn't have let him.' There was an edge of irritation in

Phin's voice as he got up to join me at the window. 'It was only a kiss, Summer, not embezzlement or industrial espionage. You should keep it in perspective. It wasn't that big a deal.'

'For you, perhaps,' I said tautly. 'You don't care about this job. You don't really want to be here. I know you'd rather be off travelling, challenging yourself…there are so many things you want to do. It's different for me. My job is all I've got.'

There was a long silence. We stood side by side, looking out of the window.

'Perhaps it's just as well Lex interrupted us when he did,' said Phin at last.

'I'll find you a replacement PA as soon as I can.'

'There's no hurry,' he said, turning away, restless again. 'I was thinking of taking off for a while. One of the crew on the Collocom ocean race has been hospitalised in Rio, and they've asked me if I could fill in on the next leg to Boston. I just heard today. I said I'd ring tonight and let them know.'

Why was I even surprised? Had I really thought he would persuade me to change my mind? Phin would never be happy to stay in one place for long.

'What about things here?'

'There's nothing urgent. The projects we've set up will keep ticking over, and if not maybe you could keep an eye on them. Otherwise I was just due to do PR stuff, and I might as well do that on a yacht. Gibson & Grieve is one of the race's sponsors, so Lex can't complain—especially not when he's taken my PA away from me!'

It would always have been like this, I realised. Me clinging to the safety of my routine, Phin always in search of distraction. It could never have worked. We were too different. Better to decide that now. Phin was right. It was just as well Lex had come in when he had.

'So…what will we say about our relationship if anyone asks?'

'You could tell everyone you got fed up with me never being around,' he suggested. 'That would ring true. Everyone knows I'm not big on commitment.'

They did. So why had I let myself forget?

'Or you could say that I wasn't exciting enough for you,' I offered. 'Everyone would believe that.'

'Not if they'd seen you take down your hair this morning,' said Phin with a painful smile.

There seemed nothing more to say. We stood shoulder to shoulder at the window, not looking at each other, both facing the fact that it was all for the best. I wondered if Phin was feeling as bleak as I was.

'Well,' I said at last, 'it looks as if it's all change for both of us.'

'Yes,' said Phin. He turned to look at me, and for once there was no laughter in the blue eyes. 'Thank you for everything you've done, Summer. I hope Lex knows how lucky he is.'

'Thank you for all the doughnuts,' I said unevenly.

'They won't be the same without you.'

I wanted to tell him that I would think of him every time I had coffee. I wanted to tell him that I would miss him. I wanted to thank him for taking me to Africa, for making me *feel*, for refusing to let me give up on my dreams. But when I opened my mouth my throat was too tight to speak, and I knew that even if I could I would cry.

'I must go,' was all I muttered, backing away. 'I'll see you before you go, I expect.'

I don't know whether it made it easier or not, but I didn't see him. He sent me an e-mail saying that he had got a flight the next day and that he'd be out of contact for a while.

'I know you're more than capable of making any decisions in my absence,' he finished. *'Enjoy your promotion—you deserve it.'*

I tried to enjoy it. Honestly I did. I told myself endlessly that it was all for the best. I had the job I'd always wanted and a salary to match. I would be able to save in a way I never had before. If I was careful, I could think about putting down a deposit on a studio at the end of the year. What more did I want?

Whenever I asked myself that, Phin's image would appear in my mind. I could picture him in such detail it hurt. That lazy, lopsided grin. The blue, blue eyes. The warmth and humour and wonderful solidity of him. The longing to see him would clutch at my throat, making it hard to breathe, and I wanted to run down the stairs, back to his office, to throw myself onto his lap and spin and spin and spin on his chair as we kissed.

But his chair was empty. Phin wasn't there. He was out on the ocean, in the ozone, the wind in his hair and his eyes full of sunlight. He was where he wanted to be.

And I was where *I* wanted to be, I reminded myself, coming full circle again. I threw myself into work, and mostly people left me alone. There hadn't been any need for an announcement. With Phin gone, and me concentrating fiercely at work, I think most people assumed that we'd split up. They eyed me sympathetically and murmured that they were very sorry. I was just glad not to have to talk about it.

It was very different working for Lex. There were no coffee breaks, no doughnuts. Lex never sat on my desk or held my stapler like a microphone or pretended to make it bite me. It would never occur to Lex to call me anything but my name, and he wasn't interested in my life outside the office.

Not that I had much of one. Anne worried about me. 'You went to all that trouble to get Jonathan back,' she pointed out. 'I don't understand why you won't go out with him now. It's not like he isn't trying. He's always asking you out, and this time he sounds serious. Look at all those hints he's dropped about getting married.'

'I don't want to marry Jonathan,' I said. 'It wouldn't be fair.'

'Because you're in love with Phin?'

I didn't even try to deny it, but there was no point in thinking about Phin. I had to be realistic.

'I do like Jonathan—I actually like him more now than I did when I was in love with him—but if I married him it would just be because he's got a steady job and is ready to settle down. That's not a good enough reason. I know that now. I've got my own steady job,' I told Anne. 'I don't want a relationship for the sake of it. I've realised that I don't need to rely on anybody else to make me feel safe. If security is what I want, I have to make it for myself. I'm earning a decent salary now, and I can think about putting down a deposit soon. I'm going to buy my own place, and then I'll be safe.'

Anne made a face. 'I know security's important to you, Summer, but don't you want more than that?'

I pushed Phin's image firmly away. 'Feeling safe will be enough,' I said.

CHAPTER TEN

OF COURSE, it wasn't that easy. It was all very well to resolve to make my own security and put Phin out of my mind, but how could I do that when he was stuck out in the wild Atlantic? I couldn't think about buying flats until I knew he was safe.

I followed the Collocom race on the internet. I knew six boats had set off from Rio, but they had run into appalling weather. One boat had lost its mast, a crew member on another had been swept overboard in gigantic waves, and I was in such a panic that I actually interrupted Lex in the middle of a board meeting to ask if he knew what boat Phin was on.

'It's not the one you think it is,' said Lex, sounding almost bored. 'Phin's on *Zephyr II*. They've gone to rescue the boat that's lost its mast.'

So he would still be out there in those waves. Offering a belated apology to the board members, who were staring at my desperate interruption, I went back to find out everything I could about the seaworthiness of *Zephyr II.* My heart was in my mouth for four more days, until I heard that the weather had eased and the battered boats were all limping towards land.

As if I didn't have enough to worry about with Phin, my mother announced that she wanted to throw up the precarious existence she had eked out with her shop in Taunton to—and I quote—'become a pilgrim along the sacred routes of our ancestors'.

How she would support herself while criss-crossing the country on ley lines wasn't clear. 'It's all part of the healing process,' she told me, brushing aside my questions about national insurance and rent and remaindered stock. 'This is important work, darling. The galactic core is in crisis. We must channel our light to restore its equilibrium.'

It seemed to me that it wasn't just the galactic core that was in crisis. Her financial affairs were in no better state, and sadly no amount of channelling was going to sort them out.

'Can you believe it?' my mother huffed incredulously when I tried to pin her down about what was happening with the shop. 'They've cut the electricity off!'

That's my mother for you. No problem at all in believing that she has a direct connection to the galactic core—whatever that is—but entirely baffled at the notion that a utility company might stop providing electricity if they're not paid on time.

Is it any wonder I couldn't concentrate on buying a flat?

And, as it turned out, it was just as well.

It became clear that I would have to go down to Somerset and sort things out for Mum. I had encouraged her to rent the shop a couple of years ago. It had seemed like something that would fix her in one place. I should have known that the enthusiasm would pass like all the others.

Things were so busy at work that there was no way I could take time off for the first few weeks, but as soon as I heard that Phin's boat had made it safely to port at the end of that leg of the race I nerved myself to ask Lex if I could have a couple of days the following week.

'Are you thinking of a holiday?'

'I'm afraid not.' I told him about my mother's shop. 'I'll probably need to talk to the bank and her landlord, otherwise I'd just try and do it all in a weekend,' I finished.

Lex looked at me thoughtfully. 'It's unfortunate for you that you're so good at sorting things out. Take whatever time you need,' he said, much to my surprise. I knew he hated it when his PA wasn't there, and he was only just adjusting to having me instead of Monique. 'Lotty will just have to steel herself to deal with me on her own.'

He turned back to his computer. 'I believe all the Collocom boats have made it to Boston,' he said. 'I imagine Phin will be on his way home soon.'

Phin. I felt the memory of his smile tingle through me. 'We're not…it was just…' I stammered, unsure how much Phin had told his brother about the agreement we had made.

Lex held up a hand, obviously to forestall any emotional confession. 'You don't need to explain,' he said. 'I'd rather not know. Have you heard Jonathan Pugh is leaving us? Parker & Parker PR have poached him. It's a good move for him,' Lex added grudgingly.

'I'll still be in London,' Jonathan said, when I

congratulated him. 'This doesn't have to be goodbye.'

He insisted on taking me out for a drink to celebrate his new job, and, once fortified by a glass of champagne, he took my hand and asked me to marry him.

'We could be so good together, Summer,' he said.

I looked at him. He was clever, attractive, successful. I had adored him once, and now…now all I could think was that he was a nice man. I remembered how much I'd loved being with him, how I'd loved feeling safe, but his touch had never thrilled me. I had never felt the dark churn of desire when I was with him. I don't think Jonathan had ever suspected I could feel desire at all until Phin had made him wonder.

I think it was then that I stopped trying to tell myself that I wasn't in love with Phin. I was, whether I wanted to be or not. I said no to Jonathan as gently as I could, and took the train to Taunton feeling as if I had let go of something I had been holding tight for too long.

I felt a strange mixture of lightness and loss— the relief of leaving something old and unwanted behind combined with the scariness of setting off on a new road all on my own again.

My mother was as vague and as charming as ever. She had got a lift into Taunton from the field where she and several others had pitched tepees in order to live closer to nature, and we had lunch together in an organic wholefoods café where tofu and carrots featured largely on the menu. I tried to get her to grasp the realities of giving up the shop, but it was hopeless.

'The material plane has so little meaning for me now,' she explained.

I sighed and gave up. I had been the one who had dealt with all the financial arrangements when she started the shop, and it looked as if I would be the one who would have to close it down.

Still, I was unprepared for quite what a muddle her affairs were in, and I had a depressing meeting with the bank manager and an even worse one with the owner of the shop, who was practically foaming at the mouth with frustration as he recalled his attempts to get my mother to pay her rent, let alone maintain the property.

'I want her out of there!' he shouted. 'And all that rubbish she's got in there, too! You clear it out and count yourself lucky I'm not taking her to court.'

Mum wafted back to her tepee, and I spent that night in a dreary B&B. I sat on the narrow bed and looked at the rain trickling down the window. I felt so lonely I could hardly breathe.

I had been so careful all my life. I had been sensible. I had been good. I had always said *no* instead of *yes*, and where had it got me? All alone and feeling sorry for myself, in a single room in a cheap B&B, with nothing to look forward to but another day spent clearing up more of my mother's mess.

I thought about ringing Anne, but she was out with Mark, and anyway she was so happy planning her wedding that I didn't want to be a misery. Besides, the only person I really wanted to talk to was Phin.

I missed him. I missed that slow, crooked smile, the warmth in the blue eyes. I missed the energy and humour that he brought with him into a room. I even missed him calling me cream puff, which just goes to show how low I was feeling.

I missed the way he made me feel alive.

Again and again I relived that last kiss. Why had I waited so long to kiss him like that? Why had I hung on so desperately to the thought of a commitment he could never give?

It seemed to me, sitting on that candlewick bedspread—a particularly unpleasant shade of pink, just to make matters worse—that I had been offered a chance at happiness and I had turned it down. I'd been afraid of being hurt, afraid of the pain of having to say goodbye, but I was hurting now, and I didn't even have the comfort of memories, of knowing that I'd made the most of the time I had with Phin.

If he ever came back to Gibson & Grieve, I resolved, I was going to go into his office, and this time I would lock the door. I would shake my hair loose and slide onto his lap again, and this time I wouldn't stop at a kiss. I wouldn't ask for love or for ever. I would live in the moment. I'd do whatever Phin wanted as long as I could touch him again, as long as he would hold me again.

I wrinkled my nose at the musty smell that met me as I opened the shop door the next morning.

I had to push against the pile of junk mail and free newspapers that had accumulated since my mother had last been in.

Depressed, I picked it all up and carried it over to the counter. Straight away I could see that someone had broken into the cash register. The only consolation was that they wouldn't have found much money. The stock, unsurprisingly, was untouched. I didn't suppose there was much of a black market in dusty dreamcatchers or vegan cookbooks.

A manual on how to make contact with your personal guardian angel was propped on display next to a pile of weird and wonderful teas. I could have done with a guardian angel myself right then, I thought, riffling through the pages with my fingers as I looked around the shop and wondered where to begin.

Coffee, I decided, dropping the book back onto the counter. There was a kettle out at the back, where the back door had been broken down. I supposed I would have to do something about that, too.

The kettle didn't work. No electricity, of course. Sighing, I went back into the shop—and stopped dead as the whole world tilted and a fierce joy rushed through me with such force that I reeled.

Phin was standing at the counter, with a takeaway coffee in each hand and a bag under his arm.

'Oh, good,' he said. 'I've found the right place at last.'

'Phin…' I stammered. He looked so wonderful, lighting up the shop just by standing there. He was very brown, and his eyes looked bluer than ever. I was so glad to see him I almost cried.

'Hello, cream puff,' he said, carefully putting the coffees down.

I still couldn't take in the fact that he was actually there. I had wanted to see him so much I was afraid I might be imagining him. 'Phin, what are you doing here?'

'Lex told me you were down here trying to sort out your mother's finances,' he said conversationally. 'I thought you could do with a hand.'

'But how on earth did you find me?'

'There aren't that many New Age shops in Taunton, but I've been round them all. I only had one more to try after this one.'

My throat was so tight I couldn't speak.

'It's nearly eleven o'clock,' said Phin, lifting the paper bag. 'I knew you'd be craving some sugar.'

'You brought doughnuts?'

'I thought that was what you'd need.'

No one had ever thought about what I needed before. That was what I had wanted most of all. To my horror, my eyes filled with tears. I blinked them fiercely away.

'I always need a doughnut,' I said unevenly.

'Then let's have these, and we can talk about what needs to be done.'

We boosted ourselves onto the counter. I'll never forget the taste of that doughnut: the squirt of jam as I bit into it, the contrast of the squidgy dough and the gritty sugar. And, most of all, the incredible, glorious fact that Phin was there, right beside me, sipping lukewarm coffee and brushing sugar from his fingers.

Only last night I'd decided that if I ever saw him again I would seduce him into a wild affair, but now that he was here I felt ridiculously shy, and my heart was banging so frantically in my throat I could barely get any words out. Typical. I didn't even know how to begin being wild.

But right then I didn't care. I only cared that he was there.

'I thought you'd still be in the States,' I said as I sipped my coffee.

'No, I decided to come straight back once we got to Boston. I got home first thing on Friday morning.'

I did a quick calculation. It was Tuesday, so he had been back four days and I hadn't known.

'What have you been doing with yourself?'

'I had things to do,' he said vaguely. 'I didn't realise you were here until I talked to Lex last night.'

And he had come straight down to help me. My heart was slamming painfully against my ribs.

'It must be a bit of culture shock,' I said unsteadily. 'From glamorous ocean race to failed New Age shop in Taunton.'

Phin smiled. 'I like contrasts,' he said.

'Still, you must be exhausted.' Draining my coffee, I set the empty beaker on the counter beside me. 'It was so nice of you to come, but there was really no need.'

'I didn't like it when Lex said you were here alone.'

'I'm fine. Taunton's not exactly dangerous.'

'That's not the point. You don't have to do everything on your own.'

But that was exactly what I *did* have to do. 'I'm used to it,' I said.

'Where's Jonathan?' said Phin, frowning. 'If he cared about you at all, he would be here.'

'I'm sure Jonathan would have come down if I'd asked for his help, but it never occurred to me to tell him about my mother. Besides,' I went on carefully, 'it wouldn't have been fair of me to ask him when I'd just refused to marry him.'

I felt Phin still beside me. 'You refused?' he repeated, as if wanting to be sure.

'Yes, I… Yes,' I finished inadequately.

My eyes locked with his then, and silence reverberated around the shop. 'Anyway,' I said, 'you're here instead.'

'Yes,' said Phin. 'I'm here.'

Our eyes seemed to be having a much longer conversation—one that set hope thudding along my veins. I could feel a smile starting deep inside me, trembling out to my mouth, but I was torn. Part of me longed to throw myself into his arms, but my sensible self warned me to be careful.

If I was going to seduce him, I was going to do it properly. The scenario I had in mind demanded that I was dressed in silk and stockings. My hair would be loose and silky, my skin soft, my nails painted Vixen. I couldn't embark on the raunchy affair I had in mind wearing jeans and a faded sweatshirt, with my hair scraped back in a ponytail.

I wondered if Phin had also been having a chat with his sensible side, because he was the one who broke the moment. Draining his coffee, he set down the paper cup.

'So, what needs to be done?'

I didn't say that he had already done everything I needed just by being there. 'Really just cleaning up and getting rid of all this stuff somehow.' I told him what the landlord had said.

Phin's brows snapped together. 'He *shouted* at you?'

'He was just frustrated. I know how he feels.' I sighed. 'I'd spent the whole day trying to deal with Mum, too. I was ready to shout myself! It's OK now, though. I've paid the rent arrears and settled the outstanding bills so everyone's happy.'

'That must have added up to a bit.' Phin looked

at me closely when I just shrugged. 'You used your savings, didn't you, CP?' he said.

I managed a crooked smile. 'It's just money, as Mum always says.'

'It was for your flat,' said Phin, looking grimmer than I had ever seen him. 'Your security. You worked for that money. You needed it.'

'Mum needed it more,' I said. 'It's OK, Phin. I'm fine about it—and Mum's very grateful. I've freed her up to get on with healing the galactic core, and the way things are going at the moment that might turn out to be quite a good investment!'

Phin's expression relaxed slightly, and I saw the familiar glimmer of a smile at the back of his eyes.

'Anyway,' I went on, 'I've decided to stop worrying so much about the future.' I smiled back at him as I jumped off the counter. 'You taught me that. I'm going to try living in the moment, the way you and Mum do.'

'Are you, now?' The smile had spread to his face, denting the corner of his mouth and twitching his lips.

'I am. You won't recognise me,' I told him. 'I'm going to be selfish and irresponsible…just as soon as I've finished clearing up here.'

Phin got off the counter with alacrity, and tossed the paper cups into the bin. 'In that case, let's get on with it. I can't wait to see the new, selfish Summer.'

I can't tell you how easy everything seemed now that there were two of us. Phin sorted everything. He left me to start packing up and went off to find a man with a van.

He was back in an amazingly short time to help me. 'Somebody called Dave is coming in a couple of hours. He's agreed to take all the stock off our hands.'

'What on earth is he going to do with it?' I asked curiously.

'I didn't ask, and neither should you. Your problem is his trading opportunity.'

We were dusty and tired by the time we had finished. Dave had turned up, as promised, and to my huge relief had taken away all the stock—which wasn't all that much once I started to pack it away. Then we'd bought a couple of brushes and a mop and cleaned the shop thoroughly, and

Phin had mended the back door where the thieves had broken in.

I straightened, pressing both hands into the small of my back. 'I think that's it,' I said, looking around the shop. It was as clean as I could make it.

Then I looked at Phin, sweeping up the debris from his repair. I thought about everything he had done for me and my throat closed.

'I don't know what I would have done without you,' I told him.

Phin propped his broom against the wall. 'You'd have coped—the way you always do,' he said. 'But I'm glad I could help.'

'You did. You helped more than you can ever know,' I said. 'You helped me just by being here. I'm only sorry to have dragged you all the way down to Somerset as soon as you got home.'

'You didn't drag me anywhere,' said Phin. 'I wanted to be here.'

I laughed. 'What? In a quiet side street of a pleasant provincial town? It's not really wild enough for you, is it? I can see you wanting to trek to the South Pole, or cross the Sahara or…or…' What *did* risk-takers like to do? 'Or bungee-jump in the Andes. But clear up an old shop in the suburbs? Admit it—it's not really your thing, is it?'

'You're not the only one who's changed,' said Phin. 'It's true that I used to be an adrenalin junkie, but it took that race from Rio to show me that I could push myself right to the edge, I could face everything the ocean could throw at me—and believe me that was a lot!—but hanging out on a trapeze over the waves in an Atlantic gale was still nothing like the rush I get when I'm with you.'

His tone was so conversational that it took me a moment to realise just what he'd said, and then I felt my heart start to crumble with a happiness so incredulous and so intense that it almost hurt.

Phin was still standing on the other side of the room, but it was as if an electric current connected us, fizzing and sparking in the musty air. I was held by it, by the look in his eyes and the warmth of his voice, and I couldn't move, couldn't speak. All I could do was stare back at him with a kind of dazed disbelief.

'I thought about you every day at sea,' he said, his voice so deep it reverberated through me. 'It was tough out there, tough and exhilarating, but as soon as we got into port all I wanted was to see you, Summer. I wanted to hear your voice. I wanted to touch you. I suddenly understood what people mean when they say they want to go home. It wasn't about being in my house, or in London. It was just being with you. And if that means spending a day clearing out an old shop, that's where I want to be.'

I opened my mouth, but no sound came out. The air had leaked out of my lungs without me noticing and I had to suck in an unsteady breath.

'I've missed you, Summer,' said Phin.

I felt my mouth wobble treacherously and had to press my lips firmly together. 'I've missed you, too,' I said, my voice cracking.

'Really?'

I made a valiant effort to pull myself together. It was that or dissolve into an puddle of tears and lust. And what a mess that would be.

'Well, apart from your fiddling, obviously.'

A smile started in his eyes and spread out over his face as he took a step towards me. 'I even missed your obsessive tidying.'

'I missed you being late the whole time.' It was my turn to take a step forward.

He came a little closer. 'I missed the way you scowl at me over your glasses.'

'I missed your silly nicknames.'

We were almost touching by now. 'I missed kissing you,' said Phin—just as I said, 'I missed kissing you.' Our words overlapped as we closed the last gap between us, and then we didn't have to miss it any more. I was locked in his arms, my fingers clutching his hair, and we were kissing—deep, hungry kisses that sent the world rocking around us.

'Wait, wait!' I broke breathlessly away at last. 'It's not supposed to be like this!'

'What do you mean?' said Phin, pulling me back. 'This is *exactly* how it's supposed to be.'

'But I want to seduce you,' I wailed. 'I had it all planned out. I was going to be your fantasy again—but this time I was going to lock the office door so that Lex couldn't interrupt us.'

Phin started to laugh. 'CP, you're my fantasy wherever you are.'

'Not dressed like this—all dirty and dusty!'

'Even now, without your little suit,' he insisted. 'You're all I want.'

Well, how was a girl to resist that? I melted

into him and kissed him back. 'That's all very well, but *my* fantasy is to seduce you properly,' I said. 'And I can't do it here.'

'I agree,' said Phin, his eyes dancing. 'If I'm going to be seduced, I'd like it to be in comfort. Does it have to be the office? Let me take you home instead. There's something I want to show you, anyway.'

So we picked up my bag from the B&B, dropped the key to the shop through the landlord's door, and headed back to London. Phin's car was fast, and incredibly comfortable as it purred effortlessly up the motorway, but I was so happy by then that I could probably have floated all the way under my own steam.

I was shimmering with excitement at the thought of what was to come, and it was still incredibly easy being together. We talked all the way back. Phin told me about sailing up the coast of South America, about winds and waves and negotiating currents, and about their dramatic rescue mission. I told him about my mother's new plan, and Anne's wedding, and how I'd decided to rent a little place on my own and not tie myself down with a mortgage.

We caught up on office gossip, too. I told Phin about Jonathan's new job. 'It's a big promotion for him.'

'Lex won't be happy, but I can't say I'm sorry he's leaving,' said Phin. 'But then, I'm just jealous.'

It was so absurd I laughed. 'You can't possibly be jealous of Jonathan, Phin!'

'I am,' he insisted. 'I remember how you felt about him. I know how important steadiness and security has always been to you. When you told me you'd talked to Jonathan in Aduaba, it seemed to me that he was offering you everything you really wanted.'

'Is that why you left when I went to work for Lex?'

He nodded. 'I thought it would be easier for you to get together with Jonathan, but as soon as I agreed to go to Rio I knew I had made a terrible mistake. All the time on the boat I thought about you with him, and I hated it. I couldn't believe how stupid I'd been. What had I been thinking? Helping you to get Jonathan back when all along I'd been falling in love with you myself. *Duh.*'

Phin slapped his forehead to make the point.

'And who had I been trying to kid with all that stuff about wanting you to be happy with Jonathan if that was what you really wanted? I was way too selfish for that. I wanted to make you happy myself, and I knew that I could do it if only you'd give me a chance. I had my strategy all worked out.'

'What strategy?' I asked, turning in my seat to look at him.

'You'll see,' said Phin. 'I flew back to London as soon as we hit land, which gave me the weekend to put the first part of my plan into action. The next stage was to find you and separate you from Jonathan somehow. So I went into the office yesterday, but of course you weren't there—and nor was Lex. I couldn't get hold of him until later, and that's when he told me you were down here on your own. I was partly outraged that Jonathan wasn't here to help you, but I was pleased, too, that you were alone so I could tell you how I felt.'

He glanced at me with a smile. 'Then you told me that you weren't going to marry him after all. You'll never know how relieved I was to hear that, cream puff.'

I smiled back at him. 'It took you going for me to realise how much I loved you,' I told him. 'I knew then that I couldn't marry Jonathan. I thought I loved him, but I didn't really know him. You were right. I loved what he represented. But you knew more about me after that first time we had coffee than Jonathan ever did. He never made an effort to see what I was really like until you made it easy for him. You were the only one who's ever looked at me and understood me. You're the one who's made me realise I can be sensible some of the time, but I don't have to be like that all the time—and I won't be when I seduce you,' I promised.

'I love the fact that you're so sensible,' Phin told me. 'I love the contrast between that and your sexiness, that you wear sharp suits but silk lingerie. And most of all,' he said, 'I love the fact that I'm the only one who sees that about you. Everyone thinks you're wonderful—'

I goggled. 'They all think I'm nitpicking and irritable!'

'Maybe, but they also know you're kind and generous, and the person they can all turn to when they need help or something has to be done. But I'm the only one that sees the cream puff in you,' said Phin, and his smile made my heart turn over.

'Don't joke,' I said, laying my hand on his thigh. 'I'm going to be channelling my inner cream puff from now on. I hope you're ready!'

Phin covered my hand with his own. 'Don't distract me while I'm driving,' he said, but his fingers tightened over mine and he lifted them to press a kiss on my knuckles.

'I've never been the kind of girl who has an affair with her boss,' I said with a happy sigh. 'I hope I'll be able to carry it off.'

'Perhaps it's just as well I'm not going to be your boss any more,' said Phin. 'We'd never get any work done. But who's going to keep me in order in the office? Have you found me a new PA yet?'

'No. Everyone I've considered has been too young or too pretty for you to share doughnuts with. I'm looking for someone who's ready to retire.'

Phin laughed. 'I won't eat doughnuts with anyone but you, I promise.'

'It's only until Monique comes back,' I said.

'I'm thinking we could get by if we look after you in Lex's office. Lotty could keep your diary.'

'Sounds good to me,' he said. 'As long as you come down to my office occasionally and lock the door before you take your hair down!'

We had been making our stop-start way along the King's Road, but now Phin turned off into his street. I looked at his house as we pulled up outside. 'There's something different… You've painted the door!' I suspect my eyes were shining as I turned to him. 'It's exactly the right shade of blue. How did you know?'

'Phew,' said Phin, grinning at my delight. 'I have to admit that was a lucky guess.'

I got out of the car, still staring. 'And window boxes!'

'I got a gardening company to do them. What do you think?'

My throat was constricted. 'It's just like my dream,' I said, wanting to cry. 'You remembered.'

'Wait till you see inside!'

I hardly recognised the house. It was immaculately clean, and all the clutter had been cleared away so that the rooms felt airy and light.

I stood in the middle of the living room and turned slowly around until my eye fell on the sofa.

Two cushions sat on it, plump and precisely angled.

I looked at them for a long, long moment, and then raised my eyes to look at Phin.

'They look all right, don't they?' he said.

Taking my hand, he drew me down onto the sofa, careless of the cushions. 'You know that studio you were thinking of renting? I was thinking you could move in here instead. I had cleaners blitz the house yesterday, so I can't promise that it will always be like this—but you could tidy up all you want.'

'Move in?' I looked around my dream house, then back to the dream man beside me, and for a moment I wondered if this really *was* just a dream. 'But aren't we going to have a passionate affair?'

'It depends what you mean by affair,' said Phin, picking his words with care.

'I mean sex with no strings,' I said adamantly. 'I don't want to tie you down. I've learnt my lesson. I want being with you to be about having fun, being reckless, not thinking about the future or commitment or anything.'

'Oh,' said Phin.

'That's what you want, isn't it?'

'The thing is, I'm not sure I do.'

I stared at him.

'I think,' he said, 'that I've changed my mind.'

My heart did a horrible flip-flop, leaving me feeling sick. 'Oh,' I said, drawing my hand out of his. 'Oh, I see. I understand.'

But I didn't. I didn't understand at all. I had just let myself believe that he wanted me as much as I wanted him. Why had he changed his mind?

Phin took my hand firmly back. 'I'm fairly sure you *don't* see, Summer. For someone so sharp, you can be very dense sometimes! I haven't changed my mind about you, you idiot. I've changed it about commitment. I've spent my whole life running away from the very idea of it,' he admitted, 'but that was because I had never found anyone or anything that was worth committing to. Now there's you, and it's all changed. It was all I could think about on the boat. It wasn't that I didn't enjoy the sailing, but this time I wanted you to come home to. I wanted to know that you would always be there.

'So I'm afraid,' he said, with a show of regret, 'that if you want to have an affair with me you're going to have to marry me. I know you're just interested in my body, but I'm so in love with you, Summer. Say you'll marry me and always be there for me.'

I looked back into those blue, blue eyes, and the expression I saw there squeezed my heart with a mixture of joy and relief so acute it was painful. I was perilously close to tears even as exhilarating, intoxicating happiness bubbled along my veins like champagne. It was like stumbling unexpectedly into paradise after a long, hard journey. It was too much, too wonderful. I could hardly take it in.

Unable to tell Phin how I felt, I reverted to joking instead.

'But what about my fantasy to seduce you?' I pretended to pout. 'I was so determined that I was going to live dangerously. You can't have an affair with your own fiancé!'

'If you want to be reckless, let's get married straight away,' said Phin.

'I don't think Lex would like that very much. He's running out of suitable PAs.'

'He'd be furious,' Phin agreed, and grinned wickedly at me. 'Let's do it anyway.'

I pretended to consider. 'I still don't get to have an affair,' I pointed out.

'How about we don't get engaged until tomorrow?' he suggested. 'Then you can have your wicked way with me tonight with no commitment at all. But I'm warning you—that's it,' he said with mock sternness as he pulled me down beneath him. 'One night is all you're going to get, and you won't even have that unless you say yes. So, just how badly do you want an affair, my little cream puff?'

'Very badly,' I said, a smile trembling on my lips.

'Badly enough to stick with me for ever after tonight?'

'Well, if I must…' I sighed contentedly.

Phin bent his head until his mouth was almost touching mine. 'So here's the deal. You seduce me to your heart's content tonight, and then we get married.'

'I get to do whatever I want with you?'

'It's your fantasy,' he agreed. 'I'm all yours. And tomorrow you're all mine.' He smiled. 'Do we have a deal?'

Well, it would have been rude to say no, wouldn't it?

I put my arms around his neck and pulled him into a long, sweet kiss. 'It's a deal,' I promised.

'Good,' said Phin, satisfied. 'Now, about this fantasy of yours…where are you going to start?'

I took hold of his T-shirt and pulled it over his head. 'I'll show you.'

MILLS & BOON PUBLISH EIGHT LARGE PRINT TITLES A MONTH. THESE ARE THE EIGHT TITLES FOR JULY 2010.

— ❧ —

GREEK TYCOON, INEXPERIENCED MISTRESS
Lynne Graham

THE MASTER'S MISTRESS
Carole Mortimer

THE ANDREOU MARRIAGE ARRANGEMENT
Helen Bianchin

UNTAMED ITALIAN, BLACKMAILED INNOCENT
Jacqueline Baird

OUTBACK BACHELOR
Margaret Way

THE CATTLEMAN'S ADOPTED FAMILY
Barbara Hannay

OH-SO-SENSIBLE SECRETARY
Jessica Hart

HOUSEKEEPER'S HAPPY-EVER-AFTER
Fiona Harper

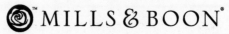 MILLS & BOON

**MILLS & BOON PUBLISH EIGHT LARGE
PRINT TITLES A MONTH. THESE ARE THE
EIGHT TITLES FOR AUGUST 2010.**

THE ITALIAN DUKE'S VIRGIN MISTRESS
Penny Jordan

THE BILLIONAIRE'S HOUSEKEEPER MISTRESS
Emma Darcy

BROODING BILLIONAIRE, IMPOVERISHED PRINCESS
Robyn Donald

THE GREEK TYCOON'S ACHILLES HEEL
Lucy Gordon

ACCIDENTALLY THE SHEIKH'S WIFE
Barbara McMahon

MARRYING THE SCARRED SHEIKH
Barbara McMahon

MILLIONAIRE DAD'S SOS
Ally Blake

HER LONE COWBOY
Donna Alward